Acclaim for Vintage

"Steve Berman has created a clever mix of urban myth, Goth, and ghost story while also tackling the confusing issues as a teen deals with his sexual orientation. *Vintage* is a clever and haunting story with some delightfully creepy scenes."

— TeensReadToo.com

"*Vintage* is an outstanding example of how genres such as YA fantasy and supernatural fiction can be used to create new stories which exploit the potential of speculative fiction to address social issues. I am already anticipating the next book by Steve Berman."

— *The Green Man Review*

"This book avoids campiness without altogether abandoning a sense of humor… Already a seasoned writer of short fiction, Berman doesn't falter in this longer tale of a predatory ghost who died young and handsome in the 1950s, the intelligent boy (with certain occult skills) who nearly falls under his spell, and a Goth girl who is more than her affectations."

— *Locus Magazine*

"There is a lot of grief, angst, anger in this story, but Berman skillfully makes it bearable with his humor and eye for detail, his ability to present interesting and appealing characters, and his compassion for the struggles and emotions of teens, especially (but not exclusively) gay teens. The horrid side of how gays are treated gets aired through memories, but we're not overwhelmed with Message…"

— Sherwood Smith, *SF Site*

"Berman wisely allows the supernatural aspects to take second seat to the real-life interactions between the narrator and his friends, and in their teenage concerns he captures the ache, longing, and frustration that makes growing up so bitterly sweet… Like its ghosts, *Vintage* may haunt you after its tale is told, holding on with its pitch-perfect depiction of adolescent hope and angst, and the ultimate triumph of love, and life, over death."

— *Edge Boston*

more…

Vintage

A Ghost Story

As Author

*Trysts: A Triskaidecollection
of Queer and Weird Stories*

As Editor

Charmed Lives: Gay Spirit in Storytelling
(co-edited with Toby Johnson)

So Fey: Queer Fairy Fictions

Magic in the Mirrorstone

Vintage

A Ghost Story

Steve Berman

Lethe Press
Maple Shade, N.J.

Published by Lethe Press, 118 Heritage Avenue, Maple Shade, NJ 08052-3018.
www.lethepressbooks.com
lethepress@aol.com

This is a work of fiction. Names, characters, places, and incidents either are the products of the author's imagination or are used fictitiously, and any resemblance to actual persons, living or dead, business establishments, events, or locales is entirely coincidental.

ISBN 1-59021-053-0
ISBN-13 978-1-59021-053-6

Library of Congress Cataloging-in-Publication Data

Berman, Steve, 1968-
  Vintage : a ghost story / Steve Berman.
     p. cm.
  Summary: A lonely seventeen-year-old who has dreamed of meeting a different and special boy desperately seeks help from his friend Trace, a Goth girl, to free him from the clutches of a handsome ghost he has met on a rural New Jersey highway.
  ISBN 1-59021-053-0
  [1. Ghosts--Fiction. 2. Homosexuality--Fiction. 3. Family problems--Fiction. 4.
Goth culture (Subculture)--Fiction. 5. New Jersey--Fiction. 6. Horror stories.]
I. Title.
  PZ7.B45423Vin 2008
  [Fic]--dc22

                                    2008001030

In Memory of
Arthur "Bob" Markus

You were the reader this book was meant for.
I can only hope that somehow
these words might reach you.

Acknowledgments

As this work evolved over several years, I owe thanks to many readers who shared their thoughts on drafts: Oliver Koble, who serialized an early version on a gay Goth Web site; Sharyn November, who offered excellent comments that added to the macabre tone of the book; Lawrence Schimel, for providing infallible career advice; Dianna Muzaurieta for criticism that honed the characters; and Greg Herren, who believed in my work and in me.

An author depends on more than help with manuscripts; writing would be a much lonelier and less bearable trade without the support of loved ones. I have to thank Theo Black, and my childhood best friend, Evan Cutler, for not letting me quit. I am grateful to Mike Thomas, who I met through working on the book; he helped me through bleak times and welcomed each chapter. My family encouraged my aspirations and ignored the growing stacks of books with which I filled the house. Without my nephew, A.J., I would never have remained sane during the final draft, as he helped with the last, troublesome revisions. My gratitude culminated with one person, my own personal Trace: Holly Black. No one has had a truer friend, no writer a better colleague, no soul a more welcome spirit, than hers. She coerced and cajoled me through the process and, when I finally sold the book, I called her first.

Chapter 1

Bored that afternoon, I was thankful when Trace suggested we attend a funeral. The September weather gave the air a wonderful crispness. At any moment I expected to shiver even though I wore a thick wool suit borrowed from the vintage clothing shop where I worked. Above me, the sky was clear except for a scattering of clouds, each a tired white against the blue.

Trace sat on the headstone next to me and slipped off her shoes to wiggle black-stockinged feet. I looked at her and felt slightly envious of how beautiful she was. Her long, black hair draped over her shoulders. She wore a sable-colored velvet dress. Even her toenails were dark; I had polished them just days ago with a bottle of cheap lacquer called "Evening's Hue." Except for a full face and the tips of her hands hidden deep into her sleeves, she might have been a shadow.

She caught me staring at her and offered a crooked smile and whispered, "Silly boy." I loved it when she called me

11

that. No guy had ever mouthed such sweetness to me except in dreams.

We both turned back to the funeral, a crowded affair down at the bottom of the cemetery slope. I counted over twenty people. Now and then someone would glance over his or her shoulder, and I wondered what they thought of us. Some strange black sheep coming to pay last respects at a distance? Lost mourners?

"Nobody dies of consumption anymore." Trace's lips pouted.

"They call it TB these days," I said.

Trace nodded. "Yeah, but that doesn't carry the same... I don't know, weight. All the cool medical terms have been left behind. 'Ague.' 'Dropsy.'" She stretched her arms wide, threatening to unbalance herself. "Doesn't that sound delicious? 'Dropsy.'"

"What did he die from?" I gestured toward the coffin below.

Trace looked at the funeral and chewed on her lower lip. Looking for a good show, she would scan the obituaries like others read the movie section. Though she mentioned this service to me yesterday, for some reason I couldn't remember how the man had died.

She shrugged and muttered, "Something modern." Her disappointment was obvious.

A leaf, gone brown and desiccated a few weeks early, blew against the old loafers I wore. I gingerly ground it underfoot. I always loved the soft crackle of autumn leaves. Every month should be filled with large piles of ochre and chocolate and rust waiting to be pounced upon.

"I never asked if you were a pine or mahogany sort of guy."

"What?" I was still distracted by thoughts of autumn.

Trace sighed in mock annoyance. "Would you want to be laid out in a plain pine wood box or something like mahogany? Elegant with brass rails and all."

I had never given my coffin much thought. Weird for someone who's often called morbid. How many seventeen-year-olds spend their time visiting graveyards? And yet I'd never envisioned my own funeral.

She let me think for a few moments—she always knew exactly how much time I needed.

"I don't suppose they make them out of glass? They could lay me out like a fairy-tale prince."

She giggled. I mock sighed as if insulted. We must have been some sight, there by the headstones, laughing loud enough to break the somber mood down below.

As the mourners walked away to their boring sedans, I stood up and stretched. Another leaf, drifting on the breeze, blew past and when I turned to follow its slow flight I caught sight of a middle-aged man, dressed as somberly as the rest. He stood at the far corner of the cemetery, by the old mausoleums. Even at a distance, I could feel his eyes staring hard at me.

When Trace took my arm, I jumped, then smiled, embarrassed. We headed down the hill, and I glanced over my shoulder. The strange man had disappeared, probably heading home himself.

Trace's battered Stanza waited for us on the street outside the cemetery gates. Stickers once covered the rear, but a few weeks ago, Trace grew bored with all the bands, sayings, and thoughts of the past year, and had me spray paint over them. The black paint stood out like a bruise against the gray primer of the rest of the car.

"Today was very quiet." She unlocked my door first.

I guess she hadn't noticed the man staring at us. I slouched in the passenger's seat, but quickly sat upright after remembering my suit was over forty years old and expensive. I ran my hand down the trousers that I had carefully ironed hours ago.

"Not the funeral. The whole day has felt subdued. Worn out." She checked her lipstick in the rearview mirror. Still perfect, her lips crimson, outlined by careful strokes of ebony liner. "Something has to happen."

"Then make it happen," I said.

"You're better at that. Remember the burial we went to back in August?"

I closed my eyes and summoned up the memory. "Was that the sweltering day when I thought I'd melt?"

"Yes. You brought along the parasol you made." She laughed. "I loved it! The black and purple lace you stitched on was mean. We drew so many stares."

"They were jealous," I said with a chuckle. But I knew no one really was jealous of me. Trace earned their attention, not me.

On the ride back to Trace's house, I kept my window open and let my hand feel the rush of the passing air. Her car threatened to stall at stoplights, so she never slowed at yellow lights and sped through intersections. She bragged about the points she'd accrued for speeding, like misbehaving behind the wheel was a game.

Her small house sat along a side street that in a few years would be overtaken by the "bad part of town." For now, it remained in suburban limbo, with a lawn blemished by brown patches and fallen shingles.

She unlocked the front door and said under her breath, "We're home, Mike." Trace believed her house was haunted. If the ghost of her older brother did exist, he had yet to answer back.

The day's mail littered the worn carpet. We walked through the sparse living room and past the kitchen to Trace's room in the back. On her door hung a beaten copper hand, a good-luck charm she picked up at some witchcraft store. In the center of the palm was an eye, the pupil an irregular piece of polished turquoise. Supposedly, it attracted good luck.

Inside, a queen-sized waterbed dominated the room and both of us fell onto the comforter and bounced, hearing the heavy smack of the water underneath. Atop the headboard I spotted a dog-eared paperback of *Tithe,* a gilded lighter, and a pack of her favorite bidi cigarettes: chocolate-flavored. They were hard to come by—she had to drive into Philadelphia for them, so she rationed them out, a couple each day.

She reached for the pack and shook out two of the small, leaf-wrapped cigarettes. I grabbed the lighter. The cheap metal felt cool in my hand.

"What are you doing tonight?" I took simple pleasure in lighting the bidi she put in her mouth, then touched mine to hers. The tips glowed a cheerful orange. With my first inhale, decadent sweet smoke blackened my throat and lungs. The warning on the pack comforted my masochistic streak.

She puffed with gentle pulls, sending scented wisps into the air. "I loaned out my copy of the latest *Weird NJ* to Kim and now she's dying to explore."

"Pass." Normally, the thought of wandering around abandoned buildings and deserted highways looking for a cheap scare would have been exciting, but I was tired of Kim's bitchy antics. She drained the fun out of everything. "Let's just hang out, sip cider, and talk."

Her lips turned down. "You have too many quiet nights. You need to get laid."

I didn't need to be reminded of my loserdom, having yet to go out on one single date or even kiss another boy. "Hunting down urban legends won't find me a boy." I drew deeply on the bidi, making the end flare for a second before turning to ash, but the taste had grown sour on my tongue. "Besides, none of the local guys would want me." She'd heard this complaint countless times.

"That's not true. You're pretty." She lightly tugged at my red-tipped bangs.

The compliment made me uncomfortable. As my best friend, she had to lie.

Trace finished her bidi—"baby joints," she once called them—and twisted back to grind the remains into the ceramic ashtray shaped like a Halloween cat's head. Mine followed a moment later.

"Stop by the shop tomorrow," I said, rising from the bed. "You can tell me how you wasted your night."

She rolled her eyes and blew me a kiss good-bye.

Passing the kitchen, I saw Trace's younger brother sitting by the table in the dark. He seemed lost in a trance, just staring into space with a forgotten sandwich on a plate in front of him.

The "second Mike" was an odd kid. Maybe being named after your dead older brother did that. Or wearing so many of his hand-me-downs. He wasn't a bad kid, but he had the knack of being annoying and underfoot.

My foot creaked on the linoleum floor and broke his spell. Second Mike turned suddenly to see me standing in the doorway. I nodded, feeling oddly embarrassed by the intensity of his gaze. Instead of his usual chatter, he lifted a hand and waved slightly. The gesture, so devoid of emotion, made me shudder.

I would have gone back to my aunt's house but my hungry stomach demanded attention and Aunt Jan's cooking was notorious. The diner a couple of miles from Trace's place was cheap—the few dollars I had left from my last paycheck would more than buy me dinner—and I savored the chance to walk for hours along a quiet highway.

The temperature dropped as the autumn sun began to set behind the trees, and by the time I reached the diner, I had decided to become a basement recluse-savant by age thirty, surrounded by stacks of newspapers with crazed penciled notes in the margins. I wanted to celebrate my fate by warming my hands around a cup of coffee.

By the time I finished a feta omelet, some toast, and my second cup, I had changed my mind. Maybe I'd reach thirty-three and then make a spectacular end with a bandolier of fireworks. On the walk back, I'd glance up at the clear night sky and imagine the explosions. Very purple blasts came to mind.

The summer when I was ten, I spent hours lying in my folks' backyard, staring up at the stars and making up new names for the constellations. I wish I could remember them.

I reached where the highway cuts through the woodlands. A light wind rustled branches. I kicked aside a beer bottle, sending it rolling to the other side of the road.

It came rolling back.

I stopped. Shivering, I looked around and noticed for the first time how ominous the woods on either side looked. The wind, I told myself. Just the wind. If Trace was with me, she'd laugh at how shaken I was. I had turned down the chance to see the secret mysteries of Jersey only to find myself all alone in the perfect setting for any number of horror movies.

I gave the bottle a savage kick, sending it off the road. The sound patched my fear. Then I heard the footfalls, so light I had to stand still and listen hard, while hoping I heard wrong. But no, they came closer. Telling myself I was all alone, that no one else would be dumb enough to be walking back to town all by themselves, I turned around. I was wrong.

The guy walked with his head down as if mindful of the wind. He looked a year or two older than me, maybe still in high school. His hands were in his pants pockets and his sweater didn't look warm enough. Even when he came closer, he kept his gaze down.

He must have been walking to or from a costume party, an early one as Halloween was weeks away. His sweater was quite the find: a green and rust-brown wool button-down with a white appliqué C. You rarely see letter sweaters anymore.

His athletic build screamed *I earned this*. The pants and shoes matched the decade too, slightly worn khakis that ended in actual penny loafers.

Since he still ignored me, I guessed he must be in a foul mood. I was tempted to ask where he'd bought the clothes. But bothering a total stranger out in the middle of nowhere would be stupid. I didn't relish the thought of getting gay bashed.

When he walked past me, I saw his face. I wanted to run after him and catch another glimpse. He was breathtaking: smooth good looks and a sharp, upturned nose, and his crew-cut blond hair left me wondering how it would feel if my fingers brushed over the top of his head.

He acted oblivious to my existence.

I don't know why I called out to him, "Cool clothes." I had never before been courageous enough around guys I thought half as beautiful as he was. Maybe the risk of provoking him was too much to resist.

The wind made my voice too loud. He stopped. I came close to running away. I thought he'd keep walking. But he turned around.

Encouraged, I took a few steps closer. I could not look away from him "It's cold out." I hugged myself for emphasis.

He nodded. The strong silent type made me nervous. Boys made me nervous. I did not know what to say, so I focused on something I knew. "I have to know. Where'd you get the clothes?"

"My clothes?" His eyes were icy blue.

"Yeah. They're hard to find, especially in such great shape. I work at a vintage shop in town."

"I've always had these."

At the time, I didn't even think it an odd response. I just wanted him to keep talking with me. I noticed the small, embroidered *Josh* in gold script on the sweater.

"Well, you should see some of the things we have down at the shop."

He glanced at me, only briefly. "I don't remember you from the party."

Party? I shook my head. "Sorry, wasn't there." I caught a faint whiff of cologne and beer before the next gust took them away from me. His odd, not-quite-detached manner made me suspect he might be drunk.

Up ahead, near Norris Street, I saw a glow. A car turned onto the highway approaching us.

"Better move." I walked onto the dirt shoulder. I didn't hear footsteps follow mine. When I turned around he was gone. Gone. Confused, I looked around, but I didn't see him. The headlights grew brighter and brighter, painful against the dark. The car streaked past.

I called out his name a couple times and wandered back and forth, sure that I had somehow missed him. Nothing. I tried to take pleasure in telling myself I had become crazy enough to imagine weird boys.

The porch light at my aunt's house was a welcome sight. I was exhausted, confused, and still shaken over seeing someone vanish. The distant sound of the television came from the den, and I walked in on my aunt sitting on the couch working on some paperwork spread out on the coffee table before her. She turned and smiled at me. "Hey, kiddo."

I gave a wave and went to my room. I had yet to decorate the walls and the closet and dresser seemed almost empty. At my folks' house, my room had been a pleasing chaos: hours of nailing and gluing strings of white lights from the ceiling like fake stars; power cords crisscrossed the corners. I had scribbled over the wallpaper with charcoal and crayons when bored, gouged into the sheetrock with knives when angry

I took my keys out of the jacket's inner pocket. They were on this cool toy I bought last October, a cheap plastic coffin with *R.I.P.* in raised letters on the clear top. Inside, rattled a tiny skeleton.

When I had decorated Trace's nails, I also blackened the key to my folks' house. It became the forbidden key, the one I'd never use again. If I hadn't run away, my folks would have thrown me out. Keeping the key served as a bitter reminder in case I weakened and felt homesick. I hadn't yet. The other keys, so bright and shiny, worked the locks in my aunt's front door. She didn't know why I left home. I made her swear not to ask my folks. I didn't know how she'd react to learning I was gay, yet I regretted keeping secrets from her. She was my favorite relative and deserved better.

I fingered the old-fashioned key next to the ones to the shop where I worked. Trace had bought the snaggle-toothed cabinet key, all dark with age, for me at the local flea market as a "welcome to town" present this past summer.

I had tossed them onto the dresser top and hung up the jacket when my aunt knocked on the door.

"C'mon in."

She opened it only wide enough to stick her head inside. "Did you eat dinner? I could throw something together for you."

"No thanks, I had a bite."

She nodded. "Okay. I'm headed out."

"Anything interesting?"

Aunt Jan shrugged. "Maybe, if I ever dyed my hair like you do," she said with a wink. She tugged at a loose curl, stared at the gray edges, and sighed. "No, I'm just going down to Atlantic City to lose some money."

"Slot junkie."

"I'm a professional." She matched my grin with a laugh.

I put away the borrowed suit, checking the trouser cuffs for smudges and the sleeves for wear. I had to take it back to the shop the next day.

In the bathroom I washed off the dark eyeliner Trace had applied for me, and stared at myself. All bony, average skin, bleh face. Why would a boy bother with me?

Back in my room, I took out the hematite rod dangling from my left ear and opened the junk drawer of the dresser. Pushing aside the bottles of nail polish—too many black and not enough weird colors—and the pile of dark ribbons and fortune cookie slips, I found the tin in which I kept the little bit of jewelry I sometimes wore. The earring looked lonesome next to a heavy necklace shedding cheap, red enamel from every link and some 12-gauge studs.

As I slipped under the covers, my thoughts strayed back to that empty highway and the strange but beautiful boy I had met that night. Ghosts aren't real. So then what happened? Try as I might to stay awake and think of an answer, I could not resist sleep.

Chapter 2

SATURDAY

I spent the morning walk to work trying to convince myself I could not have met a ghost last night. But though crazy, no other explanation made sense. I wanted the guy to be a ghost. To be different. Otherwise, I'd be afraid to talk to him again; a ghost I could handle, not someone attractive and normal.

Malvern's Olde Clothing rests near the very end of Scarborough Street. Few people ever come in to browse. Back when I started working there, the front windows were so grimy, it was hard to tell what the shop sold. Sadly, it seemed that few people in town shared my eye for vintage clothes.

As soon as I entered the shop, an eager Malvern rose to greet me. My boss reserved his afternoons for meeting chums over drinks with names like Dusty Gibson, Rob Roy, or Pisco Sour. He never looked unkempt, never staggered or acted ill-tempered like storybook drunks. My aunt once referred to him as "that dashing old boss of yours." I pieced together through brief chats that he had inherited a fortune from his family, who once owned a good portion of the town. The shop was leftover from those days, once a trendy boutique run by his mother. Malvern never needed to sell any of the stock; I think he kept the shop running more for the fond memories and something to do when not drinking highball lunches and single-malt dinners.

"Did you impress her?" Malvern pointed at the suit I carried in on a hanger.

"Who?" I asked.

"That pretty girl you're always with." He gave an exaggerated wink.

Embarrassed, I turned away. "She still looked better." Few in town knew I was gay and they were all Trace's friends. Though I'd never heard a single homophobic remark from him, men of his generation never accepted "fags." I didn't dare lose the first job I ever liked. He sipped from a mug. I doubted there was much, if any, coffee inside. "Well, there's always next time. If that 1901 suit with the rounded collar ever comes in, that'll do it. 'Course, the damned widow up in Boston could be just teasing me with it…"

"Do any business?" My asking was part of our daily routine. If I saw one or two customers a week it was a shock. I hoped Malvern would mention selling 50's clothes to a kid for a costume.

He offered the usual response, "Nothing," with a shake of his head. He put down the mug and wiped at his oiled gray mustache with a silken handkerchief. Then he puttered about for a moment, looking around, patting at the sides of his vest, before finally grabbing his fedora and beige topcoat from the wrought-iron coat rack, another antique.

"There are some new boxes the UPS fellow brought upstairs. I think they're cheap percale frocks that the college may want for some play. Best take a look. I don't really trust the dealer. Once he sent me some wool and worsted. In great shape he said, but I found moths had attacked nearly all. If they're good, unpack them and I'll price them tomorrow."

Disappointed at failing to uncover who the mystery boy was, I muttered, "I'll take care of it." Malvern must have thought it griping. I started climbing the steps, careful not to snag the suit I carried on any stray banister nails. "Should I come in early on Monday?" I tried to sound eager, so he would know how much the shop mattered to me.

"Not before ten." He tipped his hat at me and left.

On the second floor, Malvern kept the more expensive garments. A rack with clothes from the 1950s reminded me of the boy from last night.

Regretful, I returned the wool suit to the oak armoire where I kept clothes I ached to buy: a pair of elbow-length black gloves I wanted to give to Trace for her birthday; the matched set of tie and handkerchief that had my monogrammed initials; and, best of all, a bone-colored summer suit, unlined and tropical.

A sound like a swarm of giant wasps came from downstairs. The electric buzzer from the front door.

Trace balanced a black bowler on her head and looked in the floor-length mirror. "You missed a grand séance last night."

"Oh?"

"No, not really. " She returned the hat to its spot on the shelf. "Liz brought an old Ouija board on our outing. She loves to play Occultism 101."

She wasn't the only one. Anything dark and mysterious caught Trace's attention. "She should know better than to invite the expert." Books on ghosts, spirits, and even mortuary science filled my best friend's shelves. I'm not sure where she got those last few, but they're great reading when you're wasted.

Trace mock bowed, accepting the compliment. "All we found was a twisted dead tree. 'Supposed' suicide-pact lovers had carved initials all along the trunk. Dull, dull, dull. Stopping Kim from spray painting 'Lame' across the tree was more exciting than watching Liz and Maggie hand flirt over the board."

"Ah, young love." I sighed dramatically. "Any messages from Beyond for you?"

She shook her head. "The marker kept returning to the R every time."

I could imagine her frustration. "Perhaps you contacted a spirit that stutters?"

Trace met my grin. "Or R stood for revenant? So," she leaned over the counter and rubbed my arm. "Did you end up curled around your pillow the entire night?"

My turn. I fought the urge to rush through what had happened and appear nonchalant. "I think I saw a ghost last night."

Her eyes widened. "Do tell."

I smirked a little. While she stood there all expectant, I removed a crinkled twenty-dollar bill from my wallet. "Let's do take out. I'll buy if you pick up. Chicken with garlic and... hmmm... egg drop soup?"

She considered a moment, then snatched the money and returned my grin with one of her own. "Eel and California rolls for me."

Trace and I actually met over a Tim Burton film. I had been in town for just a few days when I stopped to check out the video store: A small place with much too much "family viewing" and barely anything good. I had reached out to grab *Sleepy Hollow* when someone's sigh made me turn. The girl had painted eyes. She wore this black glass-beaded choker above an old black silk nightgown. A black leather jacket shielded her from stares.

"A new boy in town. Who would have imagined? And I'm lucky to find him." She moved closer to me. "Aren't you going to say anything?" When she reached out, I thought she intended to grab my arm, but she slipped past my shoulder and took the videotape from the shelf. "Not fair." I tugged at the tape in her hand. "Don't you like to share?"

"Share?" Her giggles could intoxicate. "I love to."

I followed Trace back home; I was a puppy happy to have a new master. That afternoon, we sat close together on the shag rug in her den and watched the movie. We gorged on popcorn she had drenched in melted butter and encrusted with sugar and salt. I remember struggling over whether to comment on Johnny Depp's inherent hotness—for some silly reason I worried that Trace might think we were on a date—but I kept quiet. Weeks later she asked if I liked manga or vamp boys and I realized she had known I was gay all along.

The Palace served the best Chinese and Japanese food. Open take-out boxes, torn packets of hot mustard, and Styrofoam plates and cups crowded the counter at Malvern's. Watching Trace eat Asian food was better than television. She always kept a pair of lacquered chopsticks in her purse. Twin sticks of dark cherry wood with a stained-glasslike pattern at the end. She lifted grains of rice, bits of wasabi, and sliced ginger with a jeweler's precision. Smooth, neat, effortless.

I made do with the supplied plastic fork and still managed to spill enough to embarrass myself. "So I was walking back last night—"

She dunked a sushi roll twice into a tiny bowl of soy sauce converted from a lid. She didn't spill a drop. "I told you to come out with us."

"If I had I would never have seen him."

"True. So what happened?"

"I was coming back from the diner out on Route 47, when I heard footsteps behind me."

She lifted a hand and tapped her chin with one fingernail. "Right, it would have to be on 47…"

"Why?" Her casual reaction surprised me. Somehow, she had swiped my momentum. "What do you know?"

"No, no." Trace shook her head. "You finish first."

I hesitated but she gave me a crooked smile. "All right." I took a sip of green tea to wet my throat. "So there I was walking along an empty road when I hear someone behind me. I turn around and there's this young guy also there."

"Handsome?"

"Oh yes." My memory drifted back to every detail of his face.

"Hmmm…" I could not guess the sentiment behind her slight smile. "I've been wondering who you'd finally fall for."

"I'm not falling for him. Am I?" I pushed my food away. I wanted to talk about ghosts, not love. "He wore these awesome clothes from the '50s. I thought maybe Malvern had sold him the stuff or he found it online.

"So I wasn't sure if I should talk to him. Part of me worried how he might react. But it was late and he looked so damn cute, I had to say something."

"You're gloating."

I blushed. "He didn't seem to mind."

Trace's eyes widened. "He spoke to you?" I nodded, a bit confused. She stepped back from the counter. "Delicious!" She began to pace back and forth excitedly. "Just delicious!"

"Enough. You're obviously holding something back. Tell me."

"I know your ghost." She laughed. "Well not know him, but know of him. As soon as you mentioned 47. It's an old urban legend around here."

"I didn't think this 'burb was big enough to qualify as urban."

"Now, now. So what did he say?"

I shrugged, pretending to be apathetic. "Not much." In truth, I couldn't recall all he said and it drove me crazy. "Something about a party and being late, I think."

She nodded several times. "Makes sense."

I reached out and grabbed her hand. "Tell me."

"Well, over forty years ago a kid was killed out on that stretch of road. Run down." She lowered her voice to seem dramatic. "Some say accident. Some say not.

"Since then… well, every kid in town knows that his ghost keeps trying to get home. We all want a glimpse. Last time I was out there looking for him was back in junior high with some friends and we all hid in the woods. I fell asleep." The regret in her voice was very evident. "Still, some say they've seen him. A lot of the time they're truckers out late and pass a lonesome guy on the road. He's not in their rearview mirror. Or some lost couple stops and asks him for directions. He never speaks though. And he never reaches home." She shivered in delight at her story.

"He disappeared on me. Not long after we were talking. I turned around and he had vanished." I turned toward the shop's windows but saw only that empty highway. "I didn't want him to go."

She patted me on the arm. "Don't worry. Tonight may be different."

"Tonight?" I cracked open a fortune cookie. *Good to begin well, better to end well.* When had they stopped making actual predictions and become pithy sayings?

"Of course. We're both going back there." Trace took great care in wiping her chopsticks clean on a paper napkin. "I'll pick you up at nine?"

Instinctively, I looked at the old grandmother clock Malvern insisted on winding every other day. So many hours until then. "Okay. Well before the witching hour."

She was already at the door, stopping only to blow me a kiss. I could almost hear her thoughts, turning like gears. No doubt she'd dash home and go through all her books, preparing for tonight. I think Trace had been waiting for something like this all her life—proof that the world is not a sorry piece of shit. She wanted to know there was mystery out there.

As for me, I had been waiting my whole life to meet a boy different from the rest. Someone special. I closed my eyes, recalling last night. An afterlife spent walking the same stretch of road night after night seemed so lonely. What would it be like to be haunted?

I stared at the old clock. The hands had not even moved. It would be a long day and I wanted to see my ghost.

Trace stood by the roadside. The wind sifted through her long black hair and lifted the edges of her dark trench coat. She seemed ready to take flight at any moment.

I huddled in my worn duster sitting on the hood of the car, holding a flashlight she brought from home. With batteries near death, the beam had shrunk to a weak glow, barely more effective than the sliver of moon above.

So far, everything had been quiet and I wondered when she would lose her patience. Twice she had me shine the beam on her watch so she could see the time. I considered asking if the books ever mentioned ghosts being late but she looked so serious I didn't dare.

A yawn, sounding loud in the middle of nowhere, escaped my mouth. The caffeine from the coffee we'd drank hours ago had left my blood and I felt the first tinges of lassitude.

"Worried he might not show?" she asked, still looking out along the road.

I shook my head, unsure if she was really asking herself the question. "No; more worried I might have imagined the

Rangeview Library District
York Street
303 287-2514
05/31/18 06:49PM

Items Checked Out

Customer Number: 445021

Vintage : a ghost story /
33021025939684   Due: 06/21/18

Total Checked Out: 1
****
Renew or reserve items online
at Anythinklibraries.org

whole thing." I tried to suppress my growing doubt and the new guilt at bringing Trace out here for nothing.

Then I caught a glimpse of someone walking down the highway and I pointed. "There."

Trace turned so fast she bumped her knee on the grill of the car.

As the figure came nearer, my eyes began tearing from the growing wind and cold. We both remained quiet. I had never before felt so on edge. This was different from last night. Then, I had spoken to what I believed was just some other boy. Now I knew better. Trace must have been a storm inside, eager to prove her dreams right. One of her hands reached out and gripped my shoulder tightly. I'm not sure which of us needed steadying more.

Like a video replayed, the guy had the same stride, the same movements as last night. I think he might have walked right past us without realizing we even existed, if I hadn't slipped in front of him, blocking his way. He stopped and lifted his gaze from the road to me as if suddenly awake.

"Hey," I said, shivering all of a sudden. Maybe from the cold.

His face brightened and then he smiled. He remembered me! A sense of relief filled me and, for a brief moment, I relaxed, basking in a boy's attention. No vapor escaped his mouth when he breathed and I suddenly remembered that this boy had been dead for decades. I struggled to keep calm.

"I had to see you again," I said. Something moved on my left. Both of us turned and I saw Trace drawing closer, staring at the ghost. I had actually forgotten she was there. "It's okay, she's a friend of mine."

"Where are you walking to?" she asked him. Her voice trembled.

He never answered her. The weight of his stare left me weak. "I didn't see you at the party."

"Why isn't he talking?" Trace tugged at my arm.

I turned to her. "You can't hear him?"

She shook her head. "No. He's just standing there."

I didn't understand what was wrong, why I could talk with him and she couldn't. I became her ventriloquist dummy, repeating his simple answers to Trace, who trembled against me.

"Ask him if he remembers reaching home."

I thought that a cruel thing to ask but listened to her anyway.

All he said was, "Yes," but that managed to quicken my heartbeat. Why me? Why after all these years, had he noticed me? I suppose I should have been worried but all I felt was the sudden sense of worth he gave me.

"Were you walking back from the party last night?"

"Yes," he said softly.

"Ask him if he remembers meeting you last night."

He never answered me. Instead, he took a step back. Those beautiful eyes, a gentle blue, widened. He looked around the desolate road as if finally noticing his surroundings. He looked lost.

I took my gaze off of him for only a moment, just to chide Trace for upsetting him. When I looked back, he was gone, disappeared once more. I moaned in disgust. "We chased him away."

"I'm sorry." She walked over to where he had been standing. "They never realize they're dead. That's what the books say." She spoke fast, almost breathless with excitement. "We saw a real ghost."

"What happens when they do?

She turned toward me. "Hmm?"

"What happens when they discover they're dead?"

"Oh." Trace put a hand to her mouth a moment. "They usually fade away then."

"So you're saying we just killed him?" I looked around for any sign of him.

She frowned. "Hon, I didn't mean to ruin this for you. But, honestly, did you think something could have happened between you two?"

"Maybe not thought." My voice dropped low. "More like hoped."

"I didn't think he was your sort. Too… all American."

I closed my eyes and imagined him still standing in front of me. Josh. That had been the name on the jacket. "He was different—"

"He was a ghost. An apparition." She rubbed my back.

I turned my face so the wind would strike it. "Don't you wonder what would it have been like to kiss him?"

"Cold, probably."

I rubbed the wet corners of my eyes. How could I have let myself fall for a phantom? "I'm just sick and tired of having something so great happen to me and then it all falls apart."

Our drive back was quiet. She probably thought I was upset with her for chasing him off. Maybe I really was, I don't know. The last thing I wanted to do was talk.

"Awww…"She gave my hand a squeeze. "Don't worry. It's autumn. Everything happens in the autumn. You'll see."

I didn't bother with turning on the light switch in my room; there wasn't enough stuff to trip over. I stripped off my shirt, hearing some seam tear in protest. I angrily tossed it across the room as punishment.

As I stepped out of my jeans I noticed the open window had let in a draft. My aunt must have decided to let some fresh air into the room. Perhaps she thought it would be healthy for me. Though it was only a few feet away, I felt too bothered to close it. Instead, I collapsed on the bed, feeling sorry for myself and imagining that while I slept tonight pneumonia might slowly creep into my lungs. Then I could wake with a choking cough and live only a few short days, a bitter fantasy to discover how cold death really was.

"I'm here."

My eyes opened and I trembled at the whisper in my ear. There was more than a draft in the room with me. Or else the long hours, anticipation, and disappointment had left me exhausted and I couldn't trust my senses or my desire to see him again. I crawled to the foot of the bed. I was afraid to speak out, worried that I might be answered.

At first my eyes saw only the gloom. But a faint glow grew in a corner until I could see a pale figure standing there. The ghost of the boy from the highway took a tentative step closer. My heart beat faster though I wasn't sure if it was with fear or desire.

"I'm here. With you."

"Thank you." I could not believe I said that, even though I knew the reason he was there was because of me. For the first time in my life, I had been pursued, wanted.

I watched as he made his way to my bed. Even without much light, I could see him in detail: the sheen of Brylcreem left his hair looking wet. The way his chest filled the sweater with such promise. A slight scuff at the tips of his penny loafers. I could not stop looking at him. Knowing the risk he might suddenly disappear forced me to etch every little feature of his into my brain.

When his hand fell upon my bare arm, the feather-weight touch felt cool and set off a chain reaction of wondrous shivers through me. I fairly moaned as his fingers traced back and forth, from my elbow to my wrist.

As he touched me his voice became stronger. "I need to talk to you."

I swallowed hard. "I'll listen, Josh."

He took so long to speak again, I grew worried.

"Everything's different." He looked around my room. "This is your home?"

I nodded. It would have been too confusing to tell the truth.

"I think... I think I haven't been home in a long time." He nodded once. "I remember leaving the party. Not much else. But I never seem to come home. I'm always walking. I'm always alone." He looked straight at me, and I could see deep into his eyes, see my reflection in those ice-blue mirrors.

"I understand." I knew loneliness, the fear of being pushed away, of being left behind, of having no one.

"I hope you do." He stepped nearer. I moved back and he came even closer. "I want to stay with you."

That short-circuited my mind for a few moments. All I could think of was my aunt's reaction if I told her a ghost followed me home. And, oh yeah, we're both hot for each other, so don't mind any sounds you might hear behind closed doors.

I never answered, because he took one more step toward me and then vanished. A quick fade away to nothing, leaving me trembling and cold.

Chapter 3

SUNDAY

The air-conditioning on the dimly lit bus was broken. Sweat rolled lazily down my forehead, my back, under my arms. I tried to shift about in the seat in the hopes of finally finding the secret of being comfortable, but with the duffel bag on my lap and the person next to me leaning over more and more into my personal space, the task seemed impossible. I breathed through my mouth, disgusted at the stink of so many bodies packed tightly.

But the worst was the girl crying. I might have drifted off except for her.

She sat diagonally across from me, thin knees bent up to her chest. Her floral-print dress rode up slightly and I could see scuff marks on her knees, bruises on her shins. Her face was almost always turned toward the windows — weird because the night had made the glass into reflective mirrors — so I only caught part of her profile: thin, angular face peeking out behind limp hair. She held a tissue in a clenched fist, bringing it up to her face and down to her lap steadily.

She never stopped crying. Deep, heaving sobs that pinnacled with her shaking. High-pitched huffs and heavy groans.

I looked around the bus amazed that everyone else was fast asleep. How could they? Didn't they hear her?

I stared hard at her, wishing many evil thoughts upon her while silently begging her to just shut up so I could sleep. I'd be in New Jersey in only a couple hours.

Her hand smacked the armrest suddenly, making me jump. She turned around to look at me. All I could see were her eyes. They bled dark mascara. Empty eyes.

I woke from the nightmare with a gasp. While the bus ride to my aunt's town had been awful, and the one girl's constant crying very real, she had never looked at me once the entire trip. I was just thankful she didn't leave at the same stop. Why dream about her and not Josh?

As I stumbled out of bed, I caught a whiff of something burning. My aunt was cooking. Wearing crumpled boxers and a worn T-shirt, I made my way out into the hall, trying not to inhale the stink of something sickly sweet and charred that hung thick in the air.

In the kitchen my aunt stood by the toaster, staring at it with rapt attention. I shuffled toward her but stopped when the cool tile floor brought back the memory of Josh's touch. Twin browned remains popping up from the toaster startled us. My aunt gingerly removed whatever she had been "cooking" and dropped it onto an already full plate.

"Hey," I said softly.

She gave me a smile. "Good morning." She held up the plate overloaded with different squares. Some looked too toasted, a uniform blackish brown, others multicolored and more festive than anything I wanted to see before noon.

Needless to say, my aunt was not a chef. Convenience was her favorite ingredient. The microwave received more attention than the stove. Takeout was preferred. The fact she had bothered to take the time—even two minutes per Pop-Tart, which I figured amounted to almost a half hour's work— to make me breakfast struck me as wrong. Very wrong.

I slowly sank into one of the chairs surrounding the small kitchen table. She set the plate down right before me and the smell, a mix from some catastrophic bakery, hit me full in the face. She began rooting in the refrigerator and missed my whimper.

She brought over a carton and two glasses. I ached for coffee but a glance at the counter showed the machine sitting idle. She poured orange juice into each glass and pushed one forward. I cautiously tipped it toward me. The stuff looked too bright to be served at breakfast.

"So I thought we'd have a chat."

Damn. Chats were bad. Adults "chatted" when they wanted to tell a kid he'd done something wrong. I grabbed a Pop-Tart and started chewing; with a mouth full, I wouldn't be able to have this "chat." Gagging at the sudden taste of some nameless and artificial berry, I washed it down with a gulp of juice.

I was in hell.

"At the store I wasn't sure what flavor you'd want so I bought a variety pack. Made them all. Do you like?"

I managed to make a "Mmm" sound and forced down more of the overdone pastry.

"Try one of the chocolates." She lifted up a square decorated with icing and sniffed it twice. "Has cinnamon in it too, I think."

I nodded and drank more of the juice before taking the offered tart. Maybe the acid would dissolve the crap in my stomach so I wouldn't be too poisoned.

"So," she said, sipping from her own glass. "We never get a chance to talk. And after last night I thought it best."

"Last night?" Brown crumbs fell from my open mouth and into my glass. They attempted to float amid the pulp. Did she somehow know about my ghost?

"Yes and calm down before you choke. You're always so nervous." She casually tapped a finger on the wood. "Really, you're not half as much trouble as I thought you'd be. Nervous and quiet. Too quiet sometimes. But I never worry there'll be any trouble when I open the door. And so I rarely bother you. But—"

I sighed. There always seemed a "but" in my life. "You want me to leave?" I should have known just as things were becoming… interesting… something horrible would happen to me. What would life be like homeless?

She smiled a bit and shook her head. "Don't be ridiculous. When you showed up at my door I said you could stay." She reached over and squeezed my hand holding the glass.

"Thanks, Aunt Jan—"

"Let me finish. I never spoke to your folks about why you left them. That's your affair and I'm sure, knowing my sister, you had good reason. I'm not like her, never will be or want to be. I know you're a good kid, but I have to stress something."

I opened my mouth to speak but when she saw I had finished two Pop-Tarts she lifted up the next one on the stack and shoved it at me. Too tired to resist, I resigned myself to bitter fate and bit down on something supposed to be apple filling.

"Last night. Yeah, I know, Saturday night and you're young and there are things to do. But you're still seventeen and I just can't sleep at night knowing its past twelve and you're out there. Somewhere." She waved a hand at the window. "I need to know you're in bed. Safely home." She leaned back as if to give me more room. "That's not too much to ask."

I swallowed down the last bit of Pop-Tart. Hopefully ever. If my mother had given me a curfew, it would have been with caustic words followed by me cursing. Maybe I wasn't awake enough to argue. Or maybe I didn't want to spoil the good thing I had going, staying with my aunt Jan. She had taken me in when she could have easily just let me spend one night and then sent me off. That meant a lot to me, even if I couldn't simply come out and say so. Some instincts are too hard to overcome.

I wondered if she knew what she asked. Did Trace ever fall asleep before midnight? If so, it was only accidentally. What of the late-night rendezvous with my ghost? Yet, I wanted—no, needed—someplace calm to go when everything out there weighed me down.

"One o'clock Saturdays. Midnight every other night." I reached over and picked a garish pink pastry with sprinkles and held it out to her. "Deal?"

"Okay, deal." She brushed my hand aside. "Ugh, can't stand them."

Trace would not be up for hours so there was no sense in calling her. Still craving caffeine, I made the long walk over to DeBevec's, the only coffeehouse in town and a favorite hangout of mine. Having just opened for the day, the place was quiet.

I ordered a grandé of Nawlins blend and counted out the change, mentally squinting around the notion that payday was over a week away. The steam from the tall cup threatened to fog the horn-rimmed glasses the girl behind the counter wore.

DeBevec's lacked chairs. Instead, the owner had ransacked every last pillow and beanbag in the state to surround a few coffee tables. Except for one couple lounging at a cheaply gilded block of mahogany, the place was empty. I went to the other end of the room, kicking aside a worn lump leaking stuffing. I sank to the carpeted floor and rested my cup in my lap.

The bite of chicory nipped my tongue on the first sip. I added another packet of sugar and burned my fingertip stirring the coffee. A giggle interrupted my second taste. I glanced over the rim of the cup at the source.

The couple across the room had entwined themselves around one another. Her shoulder-length red hair poured over the side of his shaved scalp. Her legs wrapped around his, and she had one hand behind his head, nudging him forward to drink from her mug. The many silver hoops worn around her wrist jingled as they both moved. His upper lip came back stained a pale brown.

Public displays of emotion are like chicory. Seeing too much leaves me with a bitter taste in my mouth and a sour stomach. I always feel envious. Why did they have to remind me how alone I really was? The idea of romancing a ghost now seemed like a silly plot from a late-night movie.

The girl giggled again, obviously pleased with herself. I finished my cup just as they began licking hot chocolate from each other's mouths.

You can't bring a spectral boyfriend for a night out on the town or to a coffeehouse to share a mocha. Even if something happened between Josh and me, it would always be a secret.

That afternoon, I walked past Trace's house but didn't see her car parked outside. I took a chance on the town flea market. Trace enjoyed hunting for lost treasures there. I rarely went with her since the place depressed me. Everything from the food stands to the long tables of crap to the vendors themselves looked trashy and rundown.

That afternoon, a thin crowd meandered in the aisles. One old man barely had the strength to pick up a chipped plate, and a little girl no more than glanced at a bin of stripped dolls set on the tarred ground. The market was a tetanus infection's dream with all the rusty nails poking out from old wood tables and ripped cloths.

While roaming, I caught sight of Trace beside a table of shoes. I tapped her on the shoulder and she turned around, cascading long dark hair behind her and smiling when she saw me. She wore leopard-print leggings and a fuzzy black top.

She held up a single high heeled shoe, one toe decorated with a garish faux ruby bigger than my thumb.

"I have something better," I said trying to keep my voice low against the excitement filling me.

One eyebrow rose. "And that would be?" She put back the shoe. The old woman behind the table never moved. I wasn't sure she was still alive until she leaned over and spat on the ground.

"Josh." Before I could say another word, Second Mike appeared at Trace's side, his face grinning with excitement. Her little brother held in his hands a stack of old postcards and he held one up to show his sister. I caught a flash of faded handwriting on the back.

"They were only a quarter each!"

Trace smiled at me and took a proffered card. On one side a team of horses pulled a cart with some sort of crane. "Water Tower on Parade," Trace read aloud.

From the corner of my eye, I caught Second Mike staring at me. He looked away when I faced him. Trace ran a hand through his short, spiky brown hair. "So what does this make? Two hundred?"

"Two twenty-nine." He began shuffling through the cards. He unbent the corner of one.

"Want to do lunch?" I asked.

"Sure," Second Mike answered without even looking up.

Trace laughed. "I thought *you* wanted to earn millions raking leaves around the neighborhood."

Her brother made a sour face at her. "But—"

"Who wanted me to take him to the art supply store? You're not borrowing from me."

"Fine."

On the car ride to Trace's house, I felt Second Mike tug at my sleeve a moment from the backseat. I looked back and he held out one of the antique postcards. "I thought you might like this one."

I took it. On the front was a sepia-toned photograph of an old building. A burly looking man with a thick beard stood out in front on a dirt road. The sign on the building read Grace & Sons Funeral Parlor. I smiled at the macabre image and checked the back. In small cramped writing someone named Lucinda had sought forgiveness for marrying Erlton, who was buried on a Sunday.

"You sure you want me to have this?"

He nodded emphatically. "If you like it." He bit his lower lip a moment.

"It's great, thanks."

Not two seconds after Second Mike left the car and ran up to the front door, Trace put the car in gear and demanded to know who Josh was.

"The ghost."

"What, from last night?" She was overcome with laughter. "You named him Josh?"

I shook my head. "Didn't you see the name on his sweater?"

She smiled. "I must not have been paying as close attention to his... clothes as you were."

"Maybe." I felt my face burn. "Anyway, he followed me home last night."

"What?" She took one hand off the steering wheel and grabbed my arm.

Shocking her left me smug. "Surprised me, too. I was in bed when suddenly there he was. Just out of nowhere."

"And?"

"And I think he likes me." I turned on her radio. Static crackled around the local college station. "I always thought my

life would end up as an Araki film. Not something by Burton."
I never imagined any boy would ever like me.

"Josh is a good name."

I nodded. "I love names that begin with 'J.' They're perfect.
In seventh grade I had a crush on a Jared."

"Always liked Jacinth. It's an old word for hyacinth," she
said. "A gem too."

We went to the expensive supermarket and bought a small
baguette and a block of brie and sat in the parking lot getting
sticky crumbs all over ourselves. Trace made sure I left no detail
about last night unsaid.

"We should have bought figs, too." She licked a finger.
"Josh sounds wonderful for a dead jock."

I rolled my eyes at her. We had gone over this once long
ago, the sort of boy I sweated. She always thought I fell for
the wrong guys.

"So what did you buy at the mart?" While curious, I really
wanted to talk about Josh more but didn't want to be rude.
Trace was far more experienced with ghosts and boys than I
was and I wanted to know what I should do next.

Trace emptied the tote bag she always brought to the mart.
I glanced at a gilded lipstick case, a pair of twisted red candles,
and a couple of CD singles. The last object was mysteriously
wrapped in pale tissue paper.

"Oh, that's not from the mart," she murmured.

I gingerly unwrapped a small clay statuette. "Amazing.
Where did you find this?" It was a horse, at least at first glance.
But it was stained light green as much as tan and the mane was
white froth rather than hair. I turned it over and over, and with
each look I saw something new: not hooves but small fins on
the feet; a slight scale pattern on the legs; and eyes open wide
and wild.

She grinned. "My brother made it for me."

"Second Mike?"

"Uh-huh." She took it back and held it up to her face. "I told him a few days ago about this book I'm reading that has a kelpie in it. That's a mean fairy water horse. This morning when I woke up, this was on my nightstand." She pranced the clay kelpie in the air a moment. "Must have taken him all week at school."

The sculpture seriously impressed me and I lightly touched the clay with my fingers. The smooth glaze was cool to the touch, exactly how I imagined the feel of a water horse's hide. "I never knew he could make something like this. You think he could make me something?"

Trace shrugged. "You'd have to ask him."

I had said *maybe* twelve words to Second Mike, ever. But now my curiosity about him was totally piqued.

"So are you going to see him again?"

Her sudden question confused me. "What, your brother?"

"No, silly boy, your ghost."

My mood darkened. "He's not my ghost. Not yet. It's frustrating. What are the rules about dating ghosts?" I looked into her face and saw concern in her eyes and expression. "Now what?"

"I'm just wondering why *you?*"

I shrugged. "Maybe because he's gay?"

"Maybe. Just, well, I've read a lot on ghosts. Some are dangerous. Be careful, okay?"

I wanted to laugh off her worry, to call her a silly girl, but she seemed so serious. I wondered if maybe I was doing something wrong after all.

I grew restless hoping for Josh to show. Wandering about my aunt's house, I ended up in the kitchen and poured myself some spicy ginger beer. I sipped while reading the brief memos my aunt wrote on the chalkboard by the fridge. 10-23—Car needs oil change. Find pumpkin for carving. Tea lights? She had kindly written me a reminder as well. Three letters: G.E.D. I had forgotten all about that talk.

In the bathroom, I leaned against the sink and sighed at my reflection in the mirror. I hated my looks, always have. Trace was the first person to ever call me pretty. Best friends had to lie about such things. My nose looked too sharp, my hair never the way I wanted it to be, despite dyes and expensive mousse.

I opened the medicine cabinet to rid myself of the reflection. My aunt shared one trait with my mother: both never threw out any prescription, even ones that had expired in the last decade, on the hunch that one day some topical ointment, some little pill, would cure a future malady.

I wasn't so bored as to start popping. After one unsuccessful suicide attempt, I never sampled alone. Had it been four months ago? One weekend when my parents were away, I had decided the only solution to being secretly gay in a home where I wasn't wanted could be found in swallowing twelve colorful prescriptions with a glass of gin. I woke the following afternoon, disoriented and my mouth tasting nasty. My cheek next to the puddle of vomit that had saved my life. Whatever combination I had taken hadn't sat too well with me. Even days later, I had still felt unsteady, hearing voices that weren't there, catching glimpses of things that didn't exist out of the corner of my eye.

Was Josh the reason I was so anxious? I desperately wanted to see him again, even if it meant breaking curfew. I glanced at the clock and it was hours until midnight. Would he show again? I could be asleep when he did. I wasn't tired and my restlessness wasn't all because of him.

None of the thoughts in my head were comforting. They ranged from: Work. Tomorrow would be the same Monday for me as it had been for almost three months, working at the shop. Which I loved, I truly did. Malvern was a quirky but kind boss. All those wonderful vintage clothes thrilled me. Even if we never made a sale, that was fine. But the day would be identical. Hell, one day at the shop was the same as every day. A year could pass, two, three, an eternity, and it would all be the same until Malvern's liver finally stopped soaking up alcohol and he expired.

Family. Trace had been obviously proud of the kelpie figurine Mike had sculpted. Weird, I mean in some ways I'm an expert on dysfunctional families. I hate my parents. They hate me. Very simple really. Trace's father seems barely there. Her mom is institutionalized. Her older brother ran away but no one thinks he's alive anymore. Her younger brother is just odd. Yet she never says a bad word about her family. The only relative I care about is my aunt.

School. I had escaped that daily grind and should be happy. Now and then I wondered if all that arguing with my aunt convincing her to let me drop out had been the right move. Except for Trace and her few friends I knew no other kids in town by name. The thought of enrolling so late in the year was daunting. Although, at least, it would change my days, make them different, did I truly want to go back? My aunt wanted those three letters, G. E. D., in my future. I dreaded any standardized test; I wasn't standard and never tested well.

Regret and envy swirled inside of me, leaving me queasy. But more than that, I felt something strange happening. Or about to. Maybe because of my ghost. Everything else in my life had been confined to a quiet, dull routine and now Josh's appearance had changed all that. Life was now… weird. Had I always wanted it this way?

I cracked open the window and let some cool air into the room. I leaned out on the ledge, looking outside at the quiet town, the still houses. None of the stars were out and everything looked caught in mid-moment, as if also expectant.

Trace's warning came back to me. *Be careful.* Knowing she felt apprehensive scared me a little. I always trusted her, relied on her for so much. But Josh seemed sincere in his loneliness. I could see it in his eyes, hear it in that soft, gentle voice. What harm could it be to let him haunt me a while?

Chapter 4

"He never showed last night?"

Trace's voice carried weakly through the Fuji wall telephone. Malvern had brought it back from some antique hunt in Japan last winter and its square black metal case gleamed as if fresh from the assembly line. Too bad the rotary dial didn't have Japanese characters instead of numerals; that would have been cool. Still, actual bells rang inside, which made me smile whenever a call came.

"No." I drew the word out to show my disappointment. I had waited until after 2 a.m. Twice I came close to heading out to Rt. 47 to see if he was walking there, but both times stopped myself. I felt sure I had been wrong about Josh's interest. In life, he would have never paid any attention to me. Why, dead, would he be different?

Trace hesitated before speaking again. "Maybe that's for the best." In the background I could hear the other conversations around the pay phone she used at school. "So how depressed are you?"

51

"Not so bad that I'll draw dotted lines on my wrists." Truthfully, I was more resigned to being alone, that I'd not have a long enough life to try suicide again.

She chuckled. "Good. Listen, come over to my house tonight for dinner."

"Oooh, sounds like a date." I had never actually been over to Trace's for a Vaughn family dinner.

"Until tonight then, my sweet."

I spent the next hour with a needle and thread repairing a slight rip in a jacket's satin lining. I distracted myself from the pain of being stood up with thoughts of what to bring tonight. Why didn't Josh want me?

Trace greeted my knock on the door with a smile that widened as I held up a cake box. She cooed with delight. "What is it?" She tried to peek inside but the box was taped shut.

"Black forest cake, the most Gothic of desserts to be found at the local baker's."

I followed her into the kitchen. She refused my offer to help so I sat down at the table. The settings were all rough around the edges: frayed tablecloth, chipped dishes, and silverware mottled with age, but by scallop-folding the paper napkins inside each glass and using old crystal salt shakers she found at the flea market, she had made the table look ready for a banquet.

At the stove, Trace lifted a lid and the smell of something delicious with traces of garlic and rosemary spread through the house. Normally, I'm hesitant to eat anyone's cooking the first time—I'm such a picky eater—but whatever she stirred on the stovetop had me salivating and fidgeting in my seat.

Dressed in faded jeans and T-shirt that seemed a little small on him, Second Mike came walking in, his hands kneading a caramel-colored block. He gave me a pleasant, chirpy hello and sat down in the empty seat next to me.

"Put down the clay." Trace wiped her hands on a dishrag. This matronly side of Trace I had never seen before.

Second Mike glanced up at his sister. "I just started. And it's not clay," he said without whining.

"Fimo, whatever. We have company tonight."

Second Mike looked up at me. Failing to keep a smirk off my face, I stared back at him. And it must have been my night to discover new things about the Vaughn family, because Second Mike's features caught me. Why I'd never noticed how green his eyes were or given any thought to the scattering of pale freckles on his cheeks? He dropped his gaze—as if he had read my thoughts—back to the Fimo and never saw me blush.

The sound of the front door opening broke my weird new fixation with my best friend's brother. Mr. Vaughn had come home, still wearing the drab, olive-colored overalls that marked him as a mechanic from a local car dealership.

I never really talked much with Trace's dad. He always seemed distant, a tired soul who just wanted to withdraw from the rest of the world.

"'Bout fifteen minutes before it's ready," Trace said to her father as she gave a kiss to his oil-smeared cheek. He washed his face and hands in the kitchen sink. When he came to the table, his fingernails were still dark. He grunted a hello in my direction and asked me how my aunt was.

Trace cooked an amazing chicken dish with savory dark rice and steamed vegetables. Back at my folks', dinnertime equaled interrogation: my father asking what I did in school and how, my mother questioning who I spent time with and what their parents did. By the time I turned thirteen, I had developed a tightrope act, performed nightly, my answers not too long lest I be accused of "trifling" the discussion and responses not so brief that I was being curt. With my aunt, when we did find time to sit down together, there was no structure. Sometimes we'd both be reading at the table or laughing over a joke.

With Trace's family, I had expected something between these two extremes and I was right and wrong. As we all began to eat, there was actual conversation with everyone involved. Trace started by telling how they can now turn a person's cremated remains into gemstones. "They take dull carbon from the ashes and presto, you have a colored diamond."

"Not sure I'd want to wear a bit of grandma on cuff links," her father said with a laugh.

"What about Morgan?" Trace turned to me. "She was a black cat we had when I was little. I couldn't pronounce her name right so I'd always say 'Good morgin, Morgin' when I woke up."

"Back in Victorian times, they would make funeral jewelry from the hair of the dead." Mike talked with his mouth full. "Braids and locks kept inside a brooch, stuff like that."

This must be a nightly event for them. I was amazed that a family could be so congenial. My folks would *never* sit down and talk about weird things during dinner, with each person adding to the conversation.

After finishing everything on my plate, I picked up the lump of Fimo next to Second Mike. It still felt warm from his hands. "Your sister showed me the horse you made her."

"It wasn't a horse," he shot back at me.

"Right. A kelpie. It really looked great."

His hurt expression softened. "You liked it?"

I nodded. Trace chimed in, "He thought it was professional."

Second Mike blushed.

"He must have gotten it from Mother's side of the family." Mr. Vaughn held up his hands for a moment. "I can take things apart and put them back together like new, but to create something?" He shook his head. "Nah."

"So do you have more?" I held out the block.

"Yeah, in my room." When he took the clay, his fingertips brushed my hand. My skin echoed his touch.

"Can I see?" I surprised myself by asking. I mean, sure I was curious about his artwork, but in the back of my head I really was thinking I wanted to know more about *him*. I didn't really understand why I suddenly found him cute rather than annoying. Maybe it was seeing him for something other than a typical fifteen-year-old kid.

I expected Second Mike's room to be cluttered, much like his sister's, maybe with art supplies haphazardly thrown about. But his neatness surprised me. Pinned newspaper articles and old postcards decorated the walls. The floor was clear and the bed neatly made; its corners tucked in and pillows hidden beneath the comforter. Except for a couple of pictures in frames, the dresser top was clear. On a small desk lit by a tiny work lamp, he had arranged sculpting tools, lined up by length, and a rainbow array of Fimo blocks.

Second Mike had converted half of his closet into a mini gallery. Sculpture and carvings hung from tiny wires, others sat on wooden shelves or in cardboard shadow boxes: a marionette of a black swan dangled from a coat hanger, the small red bill a ruby against the dark; a miniature schooner with full sails; a cannon menaced a battalion of old wooden soldiers.

"I'm cutting the cake," I heard Trace call out.

I did not want to leave this strange new treasure trove.

"I'll bring us cake," Mike said. I nodded absently, not looking away from a horned serpent that had slithered out of myth to coil on the floor at my feet.

He came back with an old tray bearing two small plates with thick slices of black forest cake and two sweating glasses of what could only be milk. He set the tray down carefully on the desk.

When had I last drank plain milk? I sucked down half of the glass. I had to drink it fast or gag on the taste.

Second Mike tasted his milk after I had nearly finished mine. As he sipped, he closed his eyes, as if concentrating on the single act. I watched him drink, amazed at how beautiful he made it look. When he finished, I continued staring at his lips, all damp and whitewashed. I found myself leaning toward him. His eyes opened and watched me.

Trace came into the room holding two mugs of steaming coffee. "Figured you'd like some java."

I grabbed a mug from her hand, hoping that she had not glimpsed anything *about* to happen. If anything could have happened between Second Mike and me. Had I really considered kissing her brother? What was that all about? I gave him a half-smile and a shrug before following Trace back to her room.

She sat down on her bed. "Have you ever seen a ghost before Josh?"

Sipping coffee, I walked over to her bookshelf and tapped the bobble-headed Nerwin the Troll atop some paperbacks. "No. Why?"

"Just odd that he broke out of his routine for you," she said.

"Routine?"

"Ghosts are trapped spirits. They're always repeating themselves." She slipped off her shoes and flexed her toes. "Josh always walked the highway. Another ghost might only roam up and down a flight of stairs."

"So we set Josh free?"

She started to say something then shut her mouth.

"What?"

"Nothing. I just don't know what we did or how."

Thunder sounded overhead as I walked back from Trace's and I cursed not being smart enough to listen to the news and know about the weather. The wind picked up, too, tugging at me.

Trace's question of whether or not I had seen other ghosts bothered me. I think she held something back from me, but I had no idea what or why. Maybe she was finally envious of me? She had been waiting to see something like Josh for years, especially if she really did believe her house was haunted by the ghost of her older brother.

I remember asking her about Second Mike's odd name. Trace and I had been hanging around the elementary school playground at night. She had sat on the swing while I rested atop the slide with my feet dangling over the edge.

"So tell me about the First Mike."

She had remained quiet for a while. Made me nervous. I didn't know back then how much she liked to pause for dramatic effect.

"My older brother?" She swung slightly as she spoke. "I don't remember him at all, which is sad. I was a waif when he left us."

"What did he die from?"

The creaking of the old chains stopped. "That's just it, he didn't die. Or maybe he did, we don't know. He literally left us, ran away at eleven."

"Damn." My insides shuddered. Was I so different from First Mike? I had run off.

I remembered the torment the night before; I should have been sleeping but instead packed so I could leave before my parents woke. I was so afraid of what would happen when I walked out the door, not completely sure my aunt would take me. If not for her, I'd be alone. Homeless. Was that what happened to him? There had to be something wrong that made him want to go. "Why do you think he left?"

Trace shrugged. I wondered how hard it was for her to talk about First Mike. "It nearly killed my mother. She stayed in bed for days, not crying, not sleeping, just lying there in the same clothes, the same curled-up position. My father had to stay home to watch over both of us; he lost a good job because she just gave up.

"My earliest memories are all of him and the closed door of my parents' room. I would have nightmares about that door."

I slid down the slide and went over to Trace. I knelt down in the patch of sand underneath the swing and rested my head on her shin. She slid her fingers through my hair.

"About a year later my mother must have fooled them into thinking she was better, and told my father she wanted another son. I don't think he knew what she planned to do. But he should have never let her name the baby Mike again. Things got worse. She wouldn't let the baby out of her sight. She became paranoid something was going to happen to him." Trace sighed deeply. "This went on for years. He couldn't go outdoors unless she went with him. Mom even refused to let him go to nursery school. Dad finally stepped in, and she went berserk."

Which was worse, a mother who despised her son or one who was insane and smothering? Mine or hers? "What happened?"

"She had to be committed. Ancora. It's been nearly ten years since last I saw her—that's fine with me. Second Mike goes up there every so often with Dad. I think he feels responsible."

The neighborhoods I walked through were quiet at night. I saw few cars pass by. As I cut through the parking lot of a darkened strip mall, I glanced up at the windows at my huddled reflection. Lightning flashed, making the glass opaque for a second. After I blinked, I saw in the glass a faint figure standing right next to me. I jumped.

Josh's pale skin seemed to glow against the darkness. His face, his full lips, those lashes, all captured my eyes. I realized he would always stay that way, eternally beautiful. How couldn't I envy such a fate?

"I want you to come along with me." He reached out and wrapped his fingers around my hand, turning it cold.

I swallowed hard, a little frightened at his touch. "Where to?"

He smiled but remained quiet as he led me to the street.

I don't remember much of the walk, how long it took or the direction we went. Nothing we passed looked familiar, as if he found some secret route through the deserted town. I felt like I sleepwalked the entire way, noticing little other than Josh holding my hand, slowly turning my arm and side to ice. No pain, just a seductive loss of body warmth.

We stopped at a crumbling stone wall. Standing on my toes and pulling myself up with my hands, I could see over the edge. Rows of stone markers. My ghost had brought me to a cemetery.

"Why are we here?" I waited for an answer but there was none. I looked back and Josh was gone.

"Great," I muttered and started walking beside the wall until it ended in a wide gap that might have once had a gate. The paved road leading into the grounds was choked with weeds.

Another bout of thunder and lightning startled me. I caught a glimpse of someone walking through the cemetery. Josh. He must have slipped through the wall, like ghosts in movies do, and wanted me to catch up.

The graves hadn't been tended in years, which saddened me. It was disrespectful to the dead. Was it any wonder there were so many unhappy spirits out there? Some stones were overgrown or toppled and a few were scarred by vandalism. Josh moved faster than I did, but then he must know where he was headed and didn't need to worry about tripping over a fallen marker.

As I passed a row of very small headstones that had sunk into the ground, I heard soft sobs. I had lost sight of Josh. I tried to remain calm. I told myself that I had been alone in cemeteries at night before, and always felt safe and peaceful. Yet the words rang false in my head. This time felt different.

The weeping came from close by but I could not see another soul. The wind blew an acrid scent right into my face and I began coughing. The smell of smoke and something worse, like badly charred meat.

I took a few steps back, hand over my mouth, careful not to step in the patches directly in front of the little markers. The graves of children. Near the last one, the air above the headstone had grown luminous. An indistinct shape, as if captured moonlight, hovered. By its glow I could read part of the inscription. *Paul Barnes September 17, 1911—December 3, 1916.* Dead grass obscured the rest. The cries came from the light. I remained as quiet and still as possible, watching. When the spirit made no further move, my curiosity got the best of me. I slowly knelt down, keeping an eye on this new ghost, while pushing aside the brittle stalks. *Like an Ember Gone to Sky.* I looked at the other markers in the row. *Gerald. Thomas. Anna. Margolis.* All but one, the mother's, Beverly Barnes, shared the same date of death.

The stink in the air and my face and hands feeling blistering hot for a moment made me turn back. A fire. The children must have died in a blaze. I watched the spirit begin to fade away until it was all but invisible, yet the sobs remained behind a while, growing softer and softer.

My ears, though, seemed ready and open to other voices. I heard snippets of talking, whispers from the empty air.

"Josh?" I called out. My own voice sounded weak and halting.

Instantly the cemetery went quiet. Even the wind seemed to have paused. Then the shouting began; yelling, pleading, demanding, all calling out to me. I covered my ears and screamed for them to stop but they wouldn't. It only became louder, the voices more desperate. I ran but I had lost direction and wasn't sure which way was out.

My foot struck something and I pitched forward. I was lucky I didn't crack my skull open on a nearby tombstone but my hands and cheek burned where they scraped against the hard earth. Voices trailed off behind me.

I rose up and saw a pale figure with its back to me. Relief doused much of my fear. I ran over. "Josh, I'm glad I found you."

Even as I spoke, I realized the young man wasn't dressed the same. He wore an old military uniform and held a wide-brimmed hat in his hands. One second, I looked at his back, the next, he faced me. He was older than Josh, much older as far as I could tell. I screamed at the sunken cheeks and the shallow pit where the man's nose should have been. "She was so kind to me." The voice slipped through clenched teeth.

I screamed.

The ghost moved so quickly, its hand reaching out to me, the fingers slipping deep into my shoulder. I expected pain, and there was some, but mostly I felt pulled from every sensation around me. Gone was the fear, the darkness, the cold wind and the sound of thunder.

I'm lying in a hard bed, much of me under a thin sheet. Afternoon light slips in through a nearby window, but it makes everything look cold. The place stinks with sour air. Hospitals are where people come to die. It's bullshit if you think anyone walks out well from such places...

Every time I breathe in, there's an odd whistling sound... and pain, so much all I want is to stop...

A woman comes over to where I lie. She's a beautiful vision all dressed in white. The nurse. I wonder if her short blonde hair feels soft to the touch. Would her skin? I turn my head to focus on her long legs in their stockings. "Such beautiful legs," I wheeze out...

She should smile at that. Girls always smiled at a compliment from me in the past. Only, I can see something in her eyes when she looks at me now. Pity. I know the girls will never smile at me again. My hand, shaking as if palsied—at only thirty-five it should not tremble so—slips out from beneath the sheet and moves slowly up to my face. The fingernails are long and scratch my cheek. They should touch my nose but find only a ragged hole and agony...

She grabs my hand and murmurs something, her words more soothing than the morphine they give.

The ache suddenly stopped. I found myself back in the old graveyard at night. The soldier's ghost had vanished.

The memory of lying in that sickbed hadn't left me. What had just happened? I seemed to have borrowed a moment from his life, one that seemed so real it might as well have been my own. I could still smell the dying in whatever ward they had me. I leaned over and almost retched, gasping in cool night air. I said a silent apology to the grave I had nearly soiled. The marker was decorated with a nurse's cap below a name I could not make out.

When my head cleared, I stumbled on, absently touching my own face now and then to make sure it was still whole and my own. I leaned against an old tree to catch my breath and get my bearings. The bark scratched my bare neck.

I heard angry muttering from above me. I looked up and in the swaying branches right above me hung a body. The legs thrashed about. I screamed.

"What, no stomach for it?" Another ghost suddenly appeared and startled me. I could see through the scroungy young man. His ragged clothes looked turn-of-the-century. He grabbed one of the hanged man's legs. "Come on now, ol' Edward's left us coin to help."

I shook my head and watched as the ghost grinned, showing a mouth full of broken and missing teeth. He pulled down hard and I heard the crack of a neck breaking. It echoed through the graveyard.

"There now. All's well. 'Cept, I hate to be sharing." The ghost reached into his shoe and took out a knife. The blade looked very real. I swear the moonlight reflected off the metal.

He slashed at me. The knife bit into my stomach, like an icicle. I looked down and saw my shirt ripped open and blood spilling out. I clutched myself and ran. His mocking laughter filled the air.

I hid behind a mausoleum. Chest heaving, I grimaced and moved my hand aside, sure that I would see my innards slipping out. But there was no cut, no wound. My shirt and flesh were intact. My fingers still searched, having trouble believing that I wasn't injured. I didn't understand what was happening to me. Why was I seeing all the spirits and, even more frightening, why were they so intent on me?

I had to get out of there. I had taken only a few steps when I finally saw Josh. He sat on the ground, his back to a grave marker. When he saw me, he smiled. "I found myself. Looked all over last night but I finally found myself."

When he stood up I found myself reading the chiseled letters :

JOSHUA WYLE
1939-1957

Still scared, I wanted to leave the graveyard before another spirit came, but I couldn't abandon Josh. He looked so forlorn staring at his own grave. I'd stay just a little while longer. I worried that maybe freeing him from the highway had been wrong.

"You're not alone anymore." I kept my hands underneath my arms to warm the fingers. Standing so close to him made everything that much colder.

In the distance, I caught a glimpse of something pale running through the cemetery in great leaps. I shuddered, not wanting to know who or what it once was.

"I have you," he said. His words thrilled me.

"We have to leave." I whispered. The other ghosts could hear me. The sound of my voice drew them like filings to a magnet.

He stared at me intently. "Have you ever touched a boy before?"

Why did he have to say that? I blushed. The sudden image of me, no, not me, lying in bed desiring the nurse rose in my thoughts like bile in my throat. I had to focus on Josh, on how beautiful he looked and how much I wanted to be *with* him.

I nearly jumped back when Josh came to touch me. "I can barely feel you," he said softly. "I want to touch you. Deeply."

I looked into his eyes, twin pieces of blue ice. Afraid to speak, I mouthed the word "please."

He came nearer and lowered his head until his face brushed mine and it seemed as if winter pressed against my mouth and a cold gust broke through my parted lips. Such kisses break laws.

Then the clouds finally let loose. Water poured down on me, a fresh new chill to my skin. The sound deafened me and, startled, I broke the kiss to find myself alone. Damn him for leaving me alone. I wasn't even sure he was truly gone, but

I didn't dare call out. I was terrified something else might answer.

I waited as long as I could stand, shivering as the rain fell. More lightning made everything look stark, unreal with every flash. I headed back in the direction of the mausoleums, sure that the wall would be close by. If followed it, I'd eventually reach the gate. Or I could try climbing over the wall. Even if I broke an arm falling, better that than spend another minute with the dead.

But I must have gone in the wrong direction, for all I saw were more old tombstones. Water pooled on the hard earth, refusing to sink in. My feet splashed as I ran first one way and then another.

I finally caught a glimpse of a streetlamp off in the distance and used it like a lighthouse beacon to find a break in the wall. I nearly kissed the asphalt when I made it to the street.

By the time I made it back to my aunt's I was a drowned rat, soaked to the bone. I was so exhausted my mind ignored the horrors of the evening and just wanted sleep. I left puddles of water on the floor. As I peeled off the wet clothes I promised myself I would never, ever, visit a graveyard again.

Chapter 5

The interior of Trace's car smelled strongly of licorice, her favorite candy. I asked if she had spilled a bottle of sambuca. She pointed to the used tea light glued to the top of the dashboard.

"Aniseed oil keeps away coughs and colds." Guiding the steering wheel with her knees, she pulled away from my aunt's driveway and poured more oil into the empty metal shell. She breathed in deeply. "After last night, I'm not surprised you're sick."

I had overslept and felt like shit. I called Malvern to ask if I could have the day off. He told me the best way to cure congestion was bed rest and a warmed glass of rye whiskey with rock candy,

"After last night, I couldn't care less about having a cold. All those ghosts. They could hear me, Trace. I know it. As soon as I opened my mouth, they came after me. What the hell is going on?"

"Just be glad spirits don't like the rain. They can't manifest in a downpour."

I bit back a cough. The aniseed didn't seem to be helping me feel better. I reached for the small brown bottle half-filled with the oil. The tiny label read *Distillation of Pimpinella Anisum Seed 13 ml.*

"*Pimp*inella?" I tried to sound amused but my heart wasn't in the joke. I uncapped the bottle, bringing it directly under my clogged nose. Immediately the undiluted oil broke through my sinuses not unpleasantly. It reminded me of eating licorice crows with Trace during Labor Day weekend.

"I love that term. Smutty *and* scientific." Trace stopped the car on a side street. "We're here." Atop a hill squatted an immense house nearly hidden by trees with leaves the color of fire.

"Do tell."

She started up the walk, a winding series of slate steps, all crumbling at their edges. No one had bothered to sweep away the leaves and debris autumn brought to the lawn.

"So what is this place?"

Trace only winked at me. I was in no mood for theatrics and mysteries. I wanted answers, ones that would let me sleep soundly, ones that would return my life to normal.

We passed the remains of a birdbath. Half the concrete bowl lay on the ground. A raven, his feathers ruffled—I imagined from some fight with another bird or perhaps in indignation at finding the town dull—perched on the broken rim and cawed loudly as we walked by.

"Shouldn't it be flying off?"

"They get more brazen as we near Halloween," Trace remarked.

I nodded. It made sense, after all.

Just when I grew sick of climbing steps, we reached the hill-top. Ahead of us, the house lurked, an ugly beast of architecture, the sort of place that looked stooped and old, with fallen arches and creaking floors. In other words, I fell in love with it.

"Used to be a mansion. That was like eighty years ago. Then the owner willed the place to the town as the library."

"*That's* the town library?" I shook my head in amazement. "Why haven't you ever taken me here before?"

"How many books have you read since you moved here?"

Touché. "Next to none." Compared to her, I was an illiterate slob. Besides, I preferred paging through her castoffs.

A bronze placard had been bolted into the wall beside the huge wooden door that bore a wrought-iron knocker. Years of verdigris made it hard to discern all the letters. Trace pulled open the door with a grunt before I could read it.

"C'mon," she said, holding the way open for me.

Inside, the atmosphere was vastly different from wondrous autumn: the air had a still heaviness to it, as if silence had weight. I took a few steps before the door swung shut, keeping the outside world distant. The library seemed to be holding its breath, quiet, not serene but rather in suspense.

Moving through the foyer, we came to an immense redwood desk blocking our path. The librarian seated at it looked frail. Glass-enclosed bookcases were set against the far wall. To the right, a staircase with a worn runner led up. On our left was an open doorway to a parlor filled with old furniture.

We were about to head up the steps when someone called out to Trace. A man in his late forties walked out of the parlor, holding a magazine. He lifted it slightly as if to wave at us.

Trace murmured to me, "Mr. Algode, evil Math teacher." She mustered a smile and headed over to where he stood.

I leaned against the banister and admired some of the paintings along the stairwell. My back became chilled, as if someone had opened the door and let in a draft. The aniseed hadn't helped me feel any better and I began sneezing.

The librarian shushed me, bringing a spindly finger to her puckered lips. I blinked away tears brought on by the sneezes. Her head shook, her tight curls the color of dull steel. Her wardrobe with its lace collar could have been purchased in Malvern's shop but was so worn that it was almost threadbare.

"Sorry," I said in a quiet tone.

The librarian glared at me and rapped a long finger against a stack of dusty books. She lifted a pair of wire-framed glasses to her face and started reading and I sat down on the bottom step and waited for Trace. I struggled not to cough or sneeze again, my chest feeling constricted, my back aching with stress.

She came back a few moments later, though it seemed like hours, shaking her head. "Ugh, he felt the need to remind me about my algebra deficiency. Like I really care about x and y and z."

"I think she hates me," I said and nodded toward the librarian.

"Oh?" She glanced that way. "Who?"

I saw that the huge desk was empty. I couldn't think of anything reasonable to explain the woman's disappearance. Fear left me unable to do much else but reach up and squeeze Trace's hand.

"Again." My voice caught in my throat. "Another ghost."

She squatted down before me. "What? Here?"

I pulled her fingers to my cheek to warm my face.

"What's wrong with me?" I did not want to suddenly start bawling. But I was afraid. Everywhere I went I seemed surrounded by spirits. I remembered the one with the knife from last night. He had been bad; suppose the next one was worse?

"Come upstairs."

With my eyes kept low to avoid glimpses of the long-dead men and women in the paintings along the wall, I let Trace lead me by the hand to the second floor. I worried I would catch their mouths moving, as if whispering to me.

"So we need to talk about this. We can figure it all out."

But I didn't hear confidence in her voice.

We passed through an open doorway to a large reading room surrounded by shelves. After taking a step forward, I saw that old men filled every available seat in the library. I felt their yellowed eyes bore into me with spitefulness.

Trace took hold of my hand, her fingers interlacing my own. A small comfort as we took another hesitant step.

One fossil coughed, the sound of decades' worth of phlegm dislodged, brought up, examined, and then swallowed.

I wanted desperately to be away from them. How many were real? Any might be ghosts. The entire floor sounded with their creaks and groans. As we reached the stacks, my heart pounded in my chest. I wondered when this had started. How long had I been seeing spirits without knowing the truth? People on the street, in stores that I'd passed by, could all be dead. That girl on the bus, the one no one else had heard but me?

"I've come in early in the morning and those old men are always here." She shook her head slightly. "I think when they lock up and it's dark, they don't leave but sit there, waiting for something."

"Don't try and scare me." I glanced back in their direction. "There's no need."

She rubbed my back. "Old men are the least of your problems."

"Thanks."

She stopped at one shelf full of books so old that their covers had peeled away or titles worn off. She stood up on her toes, scanning the topmost titles.

"So tell me what's going on. When did I suddenly become the kid from *The Sixth Sense*?"

"Ah," she said and smiled, taking down a slender volume with brittle yellow pages. *Behind the Scenes with the Mediums*.

I held back a sneeze. "I'm surprised you haven't swiped this."

"I might today." She clutched the book to her chest, obscuring the magic eight-ball T-shirt she wore. The cover left a faint block of dust on her chest.

Anxious for her to talk to me and make things right again, I waited a while as she read until I could not stand around doing nothing. I took the first book I saw off the nearest shelf and opened it at random.

This story rather resembles the tale of a much more interesting ghost which inhabited an old manor-house in Somersetshire, and which succeeded for many years in keeping human beings out of the place. Time after time the house would be let, people always making light of its haunted reputation, or else determining to brave its terrors. But they never stayed more than a few weeks, when they invariably went away, declaring that one or more members of the household had seen an apparition on the main staircase

I stopped reading and remembered what Trace had said earlier about ghosts eternally trapped climbing stairs.

The description—and rather horrible it was—was always the same. The figure of a woman would come gliding downstairs, carrying her head under her arm, and arriving at the foot of the stairs she invariably vanished.

At last there came a tenant bolder than his predecessors, and gifted with an inquiring turn of mind. He said he liked the place and meant to stay there, and if possible evict the ghost. And he at once began to investigate. Beginning at the attics he tapped and sounded every wall and suspicious-looking board in the house, with no result in the way of discovery till he reached the principal staircase. This, being the ghost's favorite haunt, received special attention, and working his way patiently down step by step, he found at length under the old flooring at the foot of the stairs, a hollow place of considerable size. And in this hole reposed, headless, a human skeleton (which subsequent examination proved to be that of a woman) with the severed head ly-

ing by its side. Then the enterprising tenant hied him to the Vicar of the parish and told him of the grisly find, and after due consultation it was decided to collect the poor remains and bury them decently in the churchyard, a ceremony which seems to have effectually "laid" the ghost, as report says it has never since been seen.

I poked Trace. "This says by burying a ghost's remains, you lay it to rest."

Trace looked up at me. "Yeah, that works in some cases. But not all ghosts. Josh is already buried."

"Oh. Right." I started to put the book back but decided against it, thinking I should do some reading on the subject myself.

"Listen to this." As she read out loud, her finger traced the words "There have been known instances where sufferance brings about a new perception, a perlustration that sees beyond the Veil. What once was viewed as commonplace becomes unimaginable as apparitions that haunt the world on occasion are met. These *mediums* are forced to take a path little tread, between the Known World and the Gray Pale, itinerant envoys between the living and the dead."

"The Gray Pale? C'mon, that sounds silly."

She rolled her eyes. "It means that people who suffer some awful trauma and come close to death—as in your attempted suicide—can get the Sight. Ever since then you've been noticing ghosts. Hon, you're one of these mediums."

"A medium?" The word brought up images of old gypsies telling fortunes and peering into crystal balls. Flim-flam artists with friends underneath the table making knocking sounds. Bad black-and-white movies. Not at all apt for being scared shitless and threatened by ghosts everywhere you look.

"That's why Josh only hears your voice and no one else." She seemed all excited. "It's why he followed you home and all the ghosts in the graveyard were drawn to you."

"Fuck." The thought of being trendy with the dead left me queasy. I couldn't even smirk over finally being popular.

"I'm going to check this out. There's some stuff on channeling. That's what I think happened to you last night."

"More like possession." I tried not to think about it. I did not like losing myself, my identity, so easily.

"Why don't you go see if they have any old yearbooks?" She patted my chest lightly. "Bet you can find out more what your ghost was like when he was alive."

I half nodded, half shrugged. Actually, the living Josh interested me less than the dead version. Alive, he was a handsome jock, the sort that would have probably hassled me at school, laughed to my face if not behind my back. Ghost Josh, though, was different. He understood me. Hell, I *was* the only boy for him these days.

"Well, I think we should know."

"Okay, okay." I headed back to the center of the room. I managed to find a librarian who didn't frighten me, a scrawny fellow lost behind thick glasses. He was kind enough to draw me a little map.

Thick tomes in shades of green and rusty brown filled three shelves and dated back to 1940. The one I wanted from 1957 was dog-eared and taped at the corners, looking ready to die. I slowly scrutinized every photo, turned every page, distracted by all the wonderful clothes. I almost forgot what I was looking for until I saw his face again.

I found Josh in one of the early photographs, wearing the same jacket, having that same suggestion of a smile. He stood against a brick wall along with a couple of the other guys on the football team. I froze when I saw the picture, expecting the image to rise up and reform into my ghost. The page felt cool to the touch, not as much as Josh himself felt, but a reminder of him nonetheless.

He was there five times, a mark I took to mean he was popular. My favorite shot was the simple junior-class picture, with a deeper grin and hair slicked back. I became hard just thinking of him. The last one in the book had him standing next to another student, a smaller guy with sharp, handsome features. I noted how Josh's arm draped around the other boy's shoulder, the fingertips almost touching his neck. Both smiled, and Josh looked at the other boy rather than the camera. I felt instantly jealous. Last night when he asked me if I was a virgin, Josh had suggested he had far more experience. This seemed proof of that. I closed the yearbook, ready to leave.

Trace was sitting on the floor, still reading when I returned.

"How goes it, Kolchak?" I asked her.

"So-so." Trace smoothed out an errant lock of hair from in front of her eyes. "The book doesn't always make sense. Maybe the author was nuts. Anyway, he sometimes says ghosts are nothing more than memories which a medium can tap into. But then in other places he lists a whole variety of spirits." She turned a page. "Apparitions. Black dogs. Corpse candles."

"So wait, I'll be haunted by roadkill next?"

"Cute." She held out a hand for help standing up. "I wish there was more on the subject." She gestured at the stacks. "But after these two books"—she took from me the one I had looked over—"the rest are on animal magnetism, fairy faiths, and crystals. Damn it, if we lived in New Orleans, we'd have a decent occult library."

I chuckled. "If we lived in New Orleans, I'd be working on my third ghost boyfriend by now."

We ordered hot soup at the diner off Rt. 47. During the day, the patch of road where I had first seen Josh looked different: just another stretch of Jersey highway

The trip to the library had given me some answers but opened up even more questions—none of which I wanted to consider much. My head hurt, my sinuses complained. I massaged my cheeks just below the eyes.

Trace read her book. I tried with mine, but it all took place in Wales and I quickly lost interest. The paper placemat under the bowl of cream of chicken was decorated with Halloween clip art.

"Heh, that's what I want him to make me." I broke up a packet of crackers into the bowl. I stabbed at them with my spoon until they sank.

Trace looked up from the page. "Hmm?"

"Your brother. Would be cool if he made me a jack o'lantern." I glanced down at my fingers remembering the feel of the clay he brought to the dinner table. A few crumbs clung to the tips and I brushed them off.

"Sure. He'd like that."

The notion of someone bothering to make me a present was the first good thought of the day. That quickly soured though, when I realized that he'd probably make anyone who asked a sculpture. I wasn't sure why, but I wished that he'd make a special exception just for me.

Back at my aunt's house, I collapsed onto the sofa. A newspaper, open to the crossword, lay on the coffee table.. Aunt Jan had filled in only a third of the puzzle. Maybe she lost interest? Who really cares what German port city is on the Rhine or a five-letter word for tearjerker? I took up the pen and began filling the boxes with words that mattered. Josh became 33 down. Trace 12 across. I saw that 2 down started with M; without thought I filled in Mike and blackened in the final empty box so the name would fit. Then came ghost and passion and why not 1957 as well.

"What's with 1957?"

My aunt startled me. I looked up to see her reading over my shoulder.

She groaned playfully. "Have you been reading my driver's license?"

"No. Why?" I quickly pushed away the paper. "You were born in '57?"

She nodded and sat down in the recliner.

"So you've lived your whole life here, right?"

"Yeah."

"Ever hear anything strange happen? Say out on Rt. 47?"

"Has Trace been telling you about the ghost?"

I had been hoping she would say something like that. "Ghost?" I tried to act ignorant.

"Yeah, well, I guess every kid in town hears it at one time or another. It's our own little spook story. In the 50s, some high school student got run down on 47. A couple people say they've seen him walking the road. Like that legend of the 'phantom hitchhiker,' only our town ghost never stops or speaks to anyone. Just keeps walking until he disappears."

"Have you ever seen him?" My voice had dropped low, like a conspiratorial whisper.

My aunt laughed and blushed. "Well, when I was your age, some friends and I went out to 47 real late at night, hoping to see the ghost. It was a warm summer night. We hid in the bushes along the roadside. Your grandmother gave me no end of grief when she found twigs and dirt all over my clothes the next morning."

"And?"

My aunt shook her head. "We never saw anything other than a couple of deer. All that happened was we smoked a few cigarettes and finished off a bottle of Scotch Sheila Michaels swiped from her father's stash."

"Heh. Never thought of you as a wild one."

Aunt Jan gave me a little smile. "I wasn't always the up-standing citizen you know now."

"So what was the craziest thing you ever did?"

"Sounds like the truth-or-dare games I played as a kid. I guess the worst thing I ever did was steal a car." Her eyes looked out toward the bay window.

"Grand theft?"

From her unfocused gaze, I imagined she was seeing the past. "Not really. I was twenty and met this boy one summer at the shore while visiting friends. He lived in the next county and I wanted to see him after we both went home. So I borrowed your grandmother's car."

"Let me guess. This was not your normal borrowing?"

She chuckled. "Your aunt Becky was the responsible one. Your mother was the favorite. Me… your grandmother called the police when she woke and found both the car and that troublesome middle child of hers gone. I didn't even reach the county line when the police pulled me over."

"Damn." What a bitch I had for a grandmother. I didn't remember her at all; she had died when I turned four. Still, I could see where my mother's moods came from.

"Your turn. What's the worst thing you ever did?"

That was easy. But I couldn't tell her.

There was this boy who lived a block away from my folks' house. We were in the same grade and not really friends, but I hung out with him now and then. Mostly because he wasn't bad looking and had a ton of underground music burnt on CDs.

We cut school one afternoon late last spring and were hanging out in his bedroom when he pulled a few magazines out from under the cushion of a chair. I had never seen porn before. The boy tossed me one, then began leafing through another. I opened the magazine. The naked women spread wide on the page looked as though they had been airbrushed, their skin too tan, too glossy.

The other boy started talking about girls. He did that a lot. This time though he was explicit, telling me what he wanted to do with the ones in his lap. I glanced up to see him rubbing the crotch of his jeans. I blushed and looked back to the magazine, but kept on sneaking peeks at him squeezing the outline of his dick. He asked me what I thought of the girls. I shrugged and stupidly told him, "Okay, but not really my thing." He laughed at me, asking if I got off on kinky stuff. He mentioned pictures of women in high heels and shiny vinyl corsets leading men around on leashes he found online. He wondered if I wanted some girl at school to spank me and make me bark like a dog.

"No," I said, "not that." In my head, I told myself to shut the hell up.

But he went on, mentioning really demented things. Stomping mice, being swallowed by gigantic women, and even eating shit and I kept on shaking my head, totally amazed he knew about such things. Finally, he flat out asked me what I wanted.

I don't know why I told him. Maybe years of desire, feeling the need to touch and taste another boy had driven me so much to the edge that I lost all control. Or maybe I was just stupid. Without even thinking, I said, "I want to give you a blowjob."

His face fell, the skin turning gray. I knew I had made a mistake, had let my disguise fall. I stood up, the dirty magazine falling from my lap, and headed for the door.

"Faggot," I heard snarled at my back and something hard and fast hit my head above my left ear. I saw the tennis ball bounce between my feet. The first tears started to fall as I looked over my shoulder at him. He held his alarm clock ready to throw. I heard it crash against the door I shut behind me a moment later.

Afterward, I hid in my room. Sick to my stomach with self-loathing and pity. It only took four hours for all the local kids to know, two days for the neighborhood to whisper behind my back, and a week for my parents to threaten to kick me out. They told me I was a tremendous disappointment as well as a sick child. I left the very next morning. The bus station opened before my folks even woke up.

All of this went through my head in a matter of seconds. "Nothing really. Staying out all night. That's the worst." I hated lying to her. "I'm beat. I think I'll go lie down."

But I didn't sleep. Rather, I lay in bed, dressed warmly, sniffling and waiting and hoping for *him* to come. I tried to relax, yet I kept glancing back at the clock. When I yawned and saw my breath hanging in the air, the room suddenly cold, I knew he was near.

I heard his voice before I saw him. He called my name softly. I shivered in anticipation. He appeared beside the bed, close enough that he startled me. He sat down next to me, the mattress unmoving beneath him, and began teasing me, rubbing my chest. At first I could not feel his touch, but as I grew colder he seemed to gain more substance until he finally tugged up my sweater to uncover me.

I looked into that beautiful face. If being a medium, being a freak, meant that I could have someone like him, I was more than willing to risk scares from all the other spirits.

"You're mine," he whispered, his face moving close to my bare skin. My hands clutched the sheets tightly as I fought to keep still while he tickled me with his mouth below the ribs. I gasped, the touch of his lips almost painful, but delightfully so.

He gazed up at me then and smirked, looking smug and sure of himself. He moved up to my face. I remained rigid beneath him.

"You feel so warm."

When he kissed me, I forgot all about last night's embrace. This set new standards, chilling my mouth and tongue, making it difficult to breathe, an effort to talk. But I needed to tell him how he made me feel. "Josh... I could... I've never wanted anyone so much... so fast"

He chuckled. "I've heard that before."

"Oh?"

"Yes," he murmured.

Just that simple word was enough to splash cold water on the beguiling moment. Instead of another kiss, I wanted to know who else he had loved. "Tell me."

Josh shook his head and drifted toward my ear, making me tremble as he nuzzled it.

"Tell me," I said again, though much weaker.

"Roddy razzing my berries under the bleachers."

"Was he... in the yearbook..." He felt heavier atop me than moments ago. Every time I inhaled, it hurt. "That picture... was of you both?"

"Yes. Even after he took up with that sophomore from the sticks, Roddy wanted me."

I think he began licking my neck but everything felt so cold I could not be sure. Something chilled began to slip down below my waistband.

A knock on the door stopped me in mid-moan.

"Oh fuck," I muttered.

Another knock and my aunt's voice calling my name. I heard the knob rattle, maybe turning.

"No!" I cried out. My hand rose up, sinking into Josh an inch or two, I pushed him off me. With that sudden, frantic touch an eruption of new memories flooded my head.

I'm lying on the sofa in the family living room, the sound turned down on a black-and-white set so huge it dominates the rest of the furniture. Wagon Train is on the air and Roddy hates the show, doesn't understand why it is so popular, so it's easy to distract him.

He lies on the floor next to me, his head leaning back so that soft, dark hair brushes my arm. Both our pants are undone and slipped down while our hands jack each other off. I can hear his heavy breathing and know he's close. I stop and reach down to clamp my hand over his lightly haired chest, squeezing where his heart is. Roddy arches back and even though he doesn't utter a word, I can see he mouths my name. Josh. He shudders and comes and the tips of my fingers slide through the sweat and spunk on his chest.

It lasted only a moment and then I was alone in bed. The door had opened an inch before my aunt pulled it shut.

I panted, rubbing my face, feeling lost. As I rose up, a bit unsteady, I could not focus on a lie for my aunt. I kept wondering if Josh, even as he made out with me, was thinking back to Roddy.

Chapter 6

I popped a couple of cold-medication tablets as I read the note my aunt had left behind on the kitchen table. She had to attend a seminar up in Parsippany and doubted she'd be coming home that night. After what had happened yesterday, I was a bit thankful.

I called Malvern at home and he was happy to hear that I felt a bit better and would open the shop for him. He started in on a long list of packages that came in, went out, and the gripes against the local college's theater department that always wanted clothes for next to nothing.

From my aunt's house, it was only a two mile or so walk to the shop and, along the way, my mind wandered back to having Josh in bed. It had been scary and thrilling—everything and nothing like I had always dreamt.

A few blocks from the store, a boy on his bike caught my eye. His breath steaming in the cold morning and face flushed from riding fast, Second Mike braked, inches from me

"Hey," I said, surprised but glad to see him. What must it be like growing up named after a dead brother? Did he feel like a replacement? Maybe without Trace's influence, he would have ended up a freak.

As we walked, I asked him if he had sculpted anything new. That opened the floodgates. He started telling me the trick to applying the proper underglaze. Then he mentioned that in art class he had seen slides of Dutch pottery. Barely taking a breath or letting me say a word, he went off on these plates decorated with scenes from Napoleon's life. I listened, staggered more at how he spoke, an excited chatter that made his entire face shine, than at what he said. Only when he started going on about how Napoleon devised his battle plans in a sandbox, did I stop him.

"Shouldn't you be in school?"

"You're not," he said matter-of-factly.

He had me there. Back when I moved in with my aunt, I kept out of sight for a while, trying as little as possible to throw her life off track. That meant me wandering around town at all hours. Avoiding high school had been a bonus that became routine. Aunt Jan soon made it clear though it was "school or job." That next day I passed by the vintage clothing shop, took one look at the dead but elegant fashions, then stepped inside and found myself working for Malvern.

"But your sister is." I didn't add "for once."

He shrugged his bony shoulders. "One day won't matter."

We reached the shop and I took out my keys. I half-expected him to say good-bye and head off but instead he stood there on the stoop, telling me all about the stink from the fruit-fly experiment they were doing in the boring science class he was missing.

"Do you want to come inside for a while?"

He stopped in mid-sentence, swallowed hard, and hesitated a moment before nodding, as if following after me was a momentous decision.

I turned the clunky, old-style switch on the wall and the ceiling lights flickered into life. The temperature in the shop felt colder than outside and Second Mike began rubbing his arms. I moved to the thermostat, juggling the tiny lever to coax the furnace into warmth.

"Ugh, might take hours to heat up this place. I think Malvern has a space heater somewhere."

He explored while I searched for and found the small unit tucked away in the back of the utility closet. Its slightly frayed cloth-covered cord looked dangerous but I didn't want us to freeze, so I dared plugging it into an outlet. A few moments later, the heater's grill turned a welcome orange.

"Cool," I heard Second Mike say. I looked over at him admiring the mannequin in the window display. It wasn't wearing the charcoal gabardine suit and felt hat that I remembered from the other day. I almost cried out when I saw the khaki uniform, nearly identical to the one worn by the spectral soldier from the graveyard.

Second Mike never noticed my reaction. "A Vaughn fought in the war. Brady Vaughn." He dropped the sleeve of the cotton tunic. "He was a great-granduncle. I once found all my relatives dating back generations. Trace thinks I should be a genealogist or something. Not sure though." He went over to where I stood by the heater. "I mean, it doesn't sound really artistic."

I still stared at the mannequin. Malvern must have changed the display yesterday, maybe for Halloween. I wondered if he would be upset if I covered the dummy up with the moth-eaten fox fur coat kept in the back. The sight of it standing there, its back to me, was too creepy. Looking away left me nervous.

I glanced at the figure out of the corner of my eye and half-expected it to start moving.

"So what happened to Brady Vaughn?" I asked, finally realizing that Second Mike stood beside me, waiting.

"Died." Second Mike spread his hands out to the heater.

"Bullet? Cannon?"

"Arsenic poisoning treating venereal disease."

I had to laugh out loud. Second Mike blushed. His obvious embarrassment only made it worse, and I doubled over, eyes teary, almost howling.

"I'm sorry," I managed to say between remaining chuckles. "Just… that's the last thing I expected you to say."

That seemed to mollify him and he smiled back. "So what about you? Vesely's an odd last name."

"Guess so. I think it's Czech." I really didn't want to go into my family story. If I could forget about all of them but my aunt, I'd be much happier.

When I grabbed the broom, he offered to help sweep. Our eyes met and locked for more than a moment. I felt suddenly unsure of things, especially why I could feel my heart beating faster as I handed the broom over. He started cleaning the corners of the room and I pretended to busy myself organizing receipts, all the while stealing glances at him.

I understood the urge to play hooky, but why would he want to spend time here? The one possible answer that I could think of, the one that made sense, also made me a touch nervous.

Second Mike had removed his jacket. The T-shirt underneath would have been turned down by a thrift store. I considered handing over one of the fine shirts hanging nearby to see how nice he'd look wearing it.

"Guess the furnace finally woke up." He wiped some sweat from his forehead.

"Hmm? Oh yeah." I unplugged the heater. Blue sparks snapped at my fingers and I fell back onto the floor, narrowly missing electrocution. Second Mike came over and offered me a hand up. I noticed his grip stayed on me longer than necessary. When I smiled my thanks, he bit his lower lip and nodded.

"I have to go through some of the old merchandise." I motioned upstairs with a nod of my head. "If you want to help…"

"Sure," he answered quickly.

The second floor of the shop held more merchandise and a small, curtained section for changing. The third floor, really the attic, Malvern used as storage. Boxes crowded the lofty room.

"I know it looks bad."

"I've never seen so much dust in my life." Second Mike's soft voice trailed behind him as he went over to the nearest stack.

"You should look in my bedroom." Right after saying that, I realized how risqué it sounded and felt my cheeks grow warm.

I kept wiping the dust from the box tops on the knees of my jeans to keep from soiling the clothes inside. By the time I had opened and rummaged around three cartons, I looked as if I had been kneeling in oil. Sweat dripped down my face and burnt my eyes.

Second Mike came over to me, and I could not resist grinning. A coating of dust darkened his upper body. He looked down and tried to wipe away some of the grime, succeeding only in spreading it further over his clothes and arms. A faint whiff of peppermint drifted from him. He must have been chewing candy mints. When had he done that?

He leaned closer and kissed me on the lips. Sudden. Just a little kiss, no more than a cautious peck. Then the buzzer sounded, startling both of us. Of all the times for a customer to show! He gave me a sorry, almost pleading look, then dashed down the steps. I sat there a moment, stunned, trying to figure out what was happening between us.

There were still more surprises that day. Around four o'clock, Maggie walked into the shop.

I had met most of Trace's clique when we had all driven out to one of the last remaining drive-in movie theaters in the state. School had just let out for summer and Maggie reveled in the freedom. She began the night showing off her latest tattoo, a crown inside of a heart, inked onto her lower back.

At first, she intimidated me, being so open about her sexuality, unafraid to whistle at any remotely cute girl walking nearby. I had been quiet about being gay and thought only Trace knew.

That night, in the middle of the flick, some bad vampire movie, Maggie and Kim got out of the car for a snack refill and told me to come along.

A boy our age worked the concession stand. Sorta cute. As he dumped more popcorn into the bag, Kim leaned over and read his nametag.

"So, Bobby," she said, while chewing on a straw, "are you a boring guy that goes home after the drive-in closes, drinks some warm milk, and slips under the covers? Or do you like to have fun?"

He half smiled at her, looking suddenly nervous. "Uhh, sure."

I inwardly groaned and looked out at the field of cars lined up before the big screen. Trace had warned me that Kim liked attention. Maggie ignored her and knelt down to tap the glass in front of the candy. "Oooh, wish they had Valomilks."

"Well, which is it?" Kim leaned in further, no doubt to offer him a bigger view of her limited breasts through the gauzy top she wore.

"Yeah, I have fun."

"Cool, cool. So I'm thinking some snogging is long over-due."

"Snogging?" Snackboy Bobby asked.

Kim laughed. "Kissing. Heavy. Duty. Kissing. You like that sort of thing, right?" She grabbed at my shoulder and turned me around to face him, slapping me rudely on the back. "My friend here hasn't snogged a boy in ages. He's moist at just the thought of you and him."

I stood there, mortified, face burning, unable to look away at his expression of disgust.

Maggie came to my rescue. She stepped in front of me, pounding a fist onto the glass counter and making Snackboy jump. With the other hand she jabbed Kim hard in the sternum. "Thanks for reminding me there are bitches in the world," she said and grabbed my hand and led me back to the car.

Kim came back a moment later with popcorn and soda. "Too bad. You and Bobby would have made a tasty couple."

"Why the hell did you do that?" Maggie snatched the cup, tore off the lid and took a gulp.

"That was done because," Kim motioned back to the snack bar with a greasy hand, "one, he looked like a dork and you're supposed to play with guys like that." She popped a kernel and looked straight at me. "Two, I can't stand a virgin. Three, you're so scared, little boy, of telling anyone you're gay."

Maggie dumped the soda over Kim's head. The scrawny Asian girl shrieked, lifting up her arms and spilling the bag of popcorn all over herself too. Kernels stuck to her face and fingers like odd yellowed growths. "Kim, surprised you're not melting."

In the car, while an oblivious Trace watched the movie and Kim sulked while drying off with paper towels from the restroom, Maggie put her arm around me and told me that not everyone needed to be out to be proud.

Since then I've come to care for Maggie and her girlfriend Liz. It's really great to see them together—even when they fight, it's like part of some odd game that they each want the other to win.

Standing there in the shop, Maggie offered me a cheerful, "Hey kiddo." The coppery eyebrow ring she wore matched her hair. She rested her elbows on the counter, the alphabet charm bracelet on her wrist, with its silver blocks spelling K I N G, sliding down.

"What's up?"

"Same shit." She loudly snapped her chewing gum. "I thought of doing something special for Liz this Halloween."

"Aww."

"Heh, so I need a sexy costume." Maggie winked at me. "That stuff at the mall is awful, so I came here."

"Hmm." I glanced around the store then considered what we had upstairs. "You're a size ten?"

"Eleven. A flapper would be damn cool."

I went to the showier clothes that Malvern had hanging against one wall. The go-go dancer dress from the 1960s was an ugly yellow and obviously too tight for Maggie. She liked running her hands through all the fringes though. She cooed over an older dress that would fit, a strapless one in black Chantilly lace over taffeta. It looked like something an old movie starlet might wear to a cocktail dinner. But the price tag of $145 almost made her choke.

She had a few twenties in her wallet and, after scrounging through her camouflaged backpack, she found enough to bring her total to just over seventy dollars. I tried not to frown, knowing there were few full outfits she could afford.

"This is just for Liz, right? No one else will see you wearing it?" An idea had come to me.

"Nah, we're not going trick-or-treating or anything." She pulled a long, pink strand of the gum from her mouth, twirling it around her finger.

"How about a peignoir?"

"A pen-what?" She nibbled away until the gum returned to her mouth.

"Peignoir." I went to the steps. "French. It's a loose dressing gown." I started to climb. "Very sexy."

"Oh?" She called up from the foot of the stairs.

"Hold a sec," I answered. Back on the third floor, I went to one of the stacks I had sorted through with Second Mike that morning. I stopped and touched my lips and thought of him for a moment. His kiss had been so different from Josh's: nervous and rushed. I couldn't help but wonder what might have happened next.

I brought down a dusty cardboard box and set it on the counter. "Malvern told me he tried to sell lingerie a few years ago, but too many people fingering the pieces ruined them, plus there were some thefts, so he stopped." I opened the box and lifted out the topmost satin garment. "He never sold off these peignoirs. He'd be thrilled to get a decent price for them."

They came as a set, a gauzy nightgown that stopped at the knees, with a wrap of sorts that covered the shoulders and back. Several fit Maggie's figure. I thought she'd choose the silky nylon peignoir the color of coral with white lace along the neckline but she hesitated over one black and more lacy.

"Liz likes color," I suggested.

Maggie again picked up the coral lingerie. "How much?"

I looked over the sheet of paper that had been left with the lingerie. Malvern's handwriting. "Fifty." He would not complain over making a few dollars.

"How about thirty and pictures?"

I laughed and rang her up on the old cash register. I felt good helping her romance Liz. She thanked me with a hug as I wrapped up the outfit for her.

"So, Trace told me we're hanging out this week." She jangled her car keys. "You'll be there, right?"

"Definitely."

I came back to find my aunt's house dark and silent. I turned on a few lights and put the bag of takeout on the kitchen table.

"You're all alone."

Even though whispered, Josh's low voice surprised me and I jumped a little.

He stood in the hallway, dimly glowing, and every inch of him more beautiful than I remembered. The lines of his face, the curve of every muscle in his chest and arms, made me ache.

He turned and walked in the direction of my bedroom. "I've missed you," I caught him saying.

Josh waited for me beside the bed. When I moved closer, he smiled and slowly slipped to his knees. He looked up at me and I lost all ability to think. He took hold of my hand, sending shivers through me. I wanted us to stay that way all night, him on his knees before me, looking both strong and tender.

I broke everything by reaching out to caress his hair. It felt so light and soft that I could not be sure I even touched anything more substantial than smoke. But he closed his eyes and seemed to like what I did.

I yearned to grasp and pull him with me to the bed and leaned closer to let him know how I felt. His tongue in my mouth was like sucking on an ice cube. Nothing had ever tasted like him. As if my face was immersed in water, but none of it trickled down my throat.

He put his hand over my crotch and lightly squeezed. I jumped a little and then, laid my own on the back of his neck. My pulse at the wrist cooled down, sending chilled blood throughout my body.

He kissed me again and I did not pull my mouth away until every bit of oxygen had left my lungs. I envied his not needing air; I wanted to stay locked with him forever.

Josh started to unbutton his shirt. I was captivated, holding my breath until he revealed a perfect chest. Each muscle visible beneath skin like pale ivory and a vague shadow where golden hair must once have grown around the nipples and a streak heading down to his waist. My hand trembled when it reached out to touch him. Josh remained still like a statue. I worried that once more I'd be lost to his memories, as my fingers reached his skin and went forward just a fraction deeper. Not yet solid, but coming close. It felt like dipping my hand into cool, delightful water. No ripples other than the smile he gave me. I felt relief that my mind remained clear, focused on the here and now. On my ghost.

He reached out to me and lifted up the edges of my shirt, letting his touch slide up my sides. He had taken something so simple and made it so indescribably perfect that I lost my breath.

Josh then laid one hand on my chest and gently slid the other to the back of my head. I actually sighed when he started to slide his fingers through my hair; it felt like wind blowing against me. I was so hard now; I could feel how I had begun to leak, leaving my boxers cool and sticky.

"Touch you deeply," he murmured.

I nodded, not really understanding what he meant or wanted, then gasped as I felt his hand push inside my chest. A moment of pain at first contact and then a gentle thrill as he explored me. I looked down and saw his arm end at the wrist against my flesh.

He made me cry out again when his fingertips began to tap like cold drops over the outside of what must be my heart. As he began to stroke me there, I started to shake at the contact, until finally I threw myself against him, hugging him tight, feeling his entire forearm now pressed inside of me. I held onto him with white knuckles and even bared teeth, and moaned.

"Yes," he whispered into my ear.

My heartbeat slowed under his cold touch, coaxed into relaxing while I shuddered. I thought, now I know what dying is like. Beautiful Josh was killing me. But there was no fear or pain. Fuck, no. I gasped at the pleasure of being touched so intimately. Moments ago I had sprayed the inside of my pants, but the orgasm never stopped.

When I could no longer hold him, even as he became solid and whole, I collapsed onto the mattress. My flesh felt insubstantial, as if I was the ghost. Josh's arm slid out of me and I cried out hoarsely at losing that touch.

He leaned down and kissed me lightly on the lips. His mouth against mine felt odd. Warm. My limbs shook; Josh had left the cold inside of me. My teeth chattered uncontrollably.

He headed for the shadows and I wanted to cry out for him to wait, to come back and touch me again, but his touch had left me so weak that before I could find my voice again, he had disappeared and left me alone once more.

I managed to bring the blankets over me in the hopes I might get warm but I could barely feel them. The thought of falling asleep frightened me. I might never wake up.

Chapter 7

After the knock at the bathroom door, I lifted my head out of the water to catch a breath. "Trace?" I called out.

She opened the door. "Are you okay?"

Another time, I would have laughed. She looked so out of sorts, no makeup, with a dark trench coat over a flimsy cotton nightgown. My phone call at midnight had startled her but I had no choice. With my aunt gone, I needed someone there; I knew I couldn't last the night on my own.

I lay naked in an overflowing tub. Spilled water was everywhere. Her bare feet splashed on the tile floor.

Trace pulled up the wicker clothes hamper to the edge of the tub and sat down on it. "What happened?"

My arm rose up slightly but the air felt so cold against my wet skin that I quickly let it splash down. I ducked back under the water for a second to clear my thoughts. "Josh came by tonight."

"And?" She went to brush away some of the wet hair from my face but I shook my head.

"Don't. I'm still not right." A shudder went through me, spilling some water out of the tub. The last thing I wanted was to be touched.

She dipped a fingertip into the water around my shoulder and quickly pulled it back. "Fuck, that's hot!"

"It's not enough."

"Tell me what happened. Did he hurt you?"

"Yes. No. I don't know." The last words came out with a whine. I ducked my head under again. Trying to tell Trace what happened was hard to explain. How to say that I had lost some integral virginity with my ghost? How to express what it was like to have him inside of me? There was no way I could even come close to describing the sensations.

"Did he hurt you?" she repeated, her voice tinged with frustration.

"We went into the bedroom. He told me how he felt. Then we…" As the water began to turn lukewarm, my arms underneath the water started to shake, sending ripples across the surface. Soon the trembling spread to the rest of me, and I gritted my teeth and clenched every muscle to keep still.

"You didn't?" Her eyebrows rose higher than I'd ever seen. "With your ghost?"

I tried a weak grin. "Yeah, we did. Sorta." I clutched my chest beneath the water, which had grown cold again. "And I think it almost killed me. He touched me… it's like he left ice inside of me."

"We need to get you warm."

I nodded as she found some towels. I slid and almost broke my neck. She wrapped me in terrycloth. I shook less than before, but the cold remained inside me. Trace led me into the kitchen looking for something hot for me to drink. She seemed lost looking in the pantry. "Ovaltine, Hamburger

Helper, Shake 'n Bake." Her face was nearly aghast. "Where the hell does your aunt shop? Mayberry?"

"Meals around here can be scary."

She took a jar to the stovetop and filled the kettle. "Go put clothes on."

I nodded, my face a rictus with an outburst of chattering teeth. In my room, I stripped off the wet boxers and grabbed whatever clothes were close at hand, trying to cover up as much of me as possible. Two pairs of socks, briefs, sweatpants, T-shirt, and a black-dyed rugby shirt with torn sleeves.

I came out to the song of the kettle, the blanket from my bed wrapped around me. Trace poured what resembled brown chalk dust into a mug while I kept my hands inches above the hot burner. I wondered if my skin would sear if I laid a palm on the glowing coil; Trace would probably have a heart attack.

"Medicine?" I asked when she handed me the full mug.

"Bad hot chocolate."

I breathed in the steam first. It smelled sickly sweet and made me wonder if chocolate ever spoiled like milk. Froth floated atop an obscene brown liquid. I closed my eyes and chugged it down in three gulps. The ice that seemed to have coated my insides began to melt, making me feel loose and liquid under my skin.

I grunted, handing back the mug. "More." I wanted to feel my throat scald.

She held up the jar, full except for the spoonfuls she had just used. "We have enough to party all night."

I woke on the couch and found Trace asleep in the easy chair across from me. I struggled to rise from underneath all the winter blankets Trace had wrapped around me. I never thought I'd be thankful to wake up sweaty.

The thick taste of bitter chocolate ruled my mouth, and I brushed my teeth and even tongue with warm water for a good ten minutes before satisfied the awful flavor was gone.

Trace stirred as I came back into the room. She stretched a moment, then blinked. "What time is it?"

I glanced at the glowing numbers of the cable box. "Just after two."

"Feeling better?"

"Yeah." A partial lie. I felt weak but no longer cold. "Thanks for coming over."

She smiled. "Any time." She wiped the sleep from her eyes. "So, what now?"

I shrugged. I could see the mess we had left in the kitchen. "I have to clean this place up before my aunt comes back."

"No, about Josh," she said.

"Oh." I collapsed onto the sofa. The fear returned. The memory of almost drowning myself in a scalding bath to feel human. "I don't want to be alone."

"Maybe… maybe we should find some way to keep him away from you?" She headed toward the bathroom. "Exorcism?"

"It's more than Josh I'm scared of." I called out to her.

She came back in a few moments shaking her head. "It looks like a flood in there."

"It's me. Even now, I can't forget how he made me feel." I lightly touched my chest over my heart where his fingers had once been. "I want that again. Part of me wants to feel him inside me again. I tell myself, next time I'll be careful and it won't get as bad." I shivered thinking about Josh inside me. Did junkies feel this way, so soon after the fix wore off? Even a bad one? Did they yearn for another?

"Hon, what little gay boy doesn't say that after he gets laid for the first time?"

"Evil." I didn't find her joke the least bit funny.

She came over to me and ran a hand through my hair. "I'll call people. We can go over to Liz's house tonight. I won't leave you alone."

I nodded but kept silent. And afterward when she dropped me back home? What then?

The brick walkway leading up to Liz's house was bordered by sleeping rosebushes on wrought-iron trellises. As Trace climbed the front steps I hung back for a moment to finger one closed blossom, feeling the yellow petal's softness. I nearly caught the edge of a thorn.

"Trace!" Liz opened the door all the way. When she looked over Trace's shoulder to see me standing there, she smiled. "And you brought your sister."

I rolled my eyes at Trace, who laughed. "Hey, Liz. Nice glitter."

Sparkling green surrounded Liz's dark eyes, perhaps a whole jar of glitter used, but it matched the emerald hue of the silk top she wore.

"You okay?" Liz asked in the midst of giving me a quick hug. "You look a little unsteady."

"Yeah." I had spent the day cleaning the house and then went under a hot shower. Yet, as soon as I stepped out of the house and saw how dark it looked outside, even wearing layers of fresh clothing seemed little protection from the cold night. I felt on edge.

"Tonight's going to be special. I can feel it." She wrapped an arm around Trace and led us deeper into the house toward the living room.

Liz's folks had abandoned her in favor of money. Earning it and spending it. They were rarely at home, going either on business trips or on vacation without her. Liz hated being left alone in the huge house.

From the spacious living room, I heard Maggie call out to us. She met us with a wide grin then stuck out her tongue for all to see the shiny new barbell.

"She's been doing that for hours," Liz chided.

"When did you get that done?" Trace said as she took her place on an overstuffed chair. Wearing all black except for the pink rhinestones on her shirt that spelled out *Kitty Slut*, she contrasted with the ivory fabric of the seat like a silhouette.

"Right after school," Maggie answered her.

I lay down at Trace's feet. If I wore a leash and dog collar, I would have looked, maybe even felt, like a happy pet.

Across the room, Kim squatted in front of the stereo, picking apart the CD racks flanking it. "With all your money, Liz, you'd think you'd buy some new CDs. These are the same shit ones you always have." She threw down the jewel case she held in her hands.

We all ignored Kim. I'm not sure whether any of us really liked her or simply tolerated her. I think she and Liz had been close in elementary school and the friendship had been dying a slow death ever since. To make matters worse, lately Kim began copying Maggie's "in your face" style. Only, with her, it turned out wrong, leaving us a little girl with a bad haircut and an attitude.

"So," Maggie said, clicking the barbell against her teeth and glossy lips. "Envious?"

"Not at all," Trace told Maggie.

We both had the antiquated single holes in each earlobe because Trace considered piercings unattractive on the terminally pale.

"Well, if you change your mind, Taylor works in this great place on South Street."

"Taylor?" Trace and I exchanged confused looks.

Both girls smiled. "Oh." Liz purred out the syllable to almost a full minute. "That's right, you haven't met Taylor yet. We found him all alone and thought he might like to have some fun with us."

Kim called out, "His stint in juvenile is over."

"Damn, you're proud of that." A deep and richly masculine voice came from the kitchen. "You'll next want me to use words like 'shiv.'"

The guy peeked into the room. His brown hair was split down the middle and hung almost to his jaw. The gleam of countless gold loops spread out on his eyebrows, in his nose, and along his ears, mixed with smooth skin the color of mocha. A stud glittered under his lower lip above a thinly trimmed beard. He wore a metal-band T-shirt and tight pleather pants, the first person I'd ever seen able to make them look good.

I felt a nudge along the small of my back. Trace's velvet shoe. I pushed back against her—my way to agree with her assessment of this Taylor. He seemed very… noticeable.

The new boy slipped back into the kitchen. There was a clinking sound and Taylor returned carrying Liz's mother's good silver tray loaded with an assortment of glasses, all filled with bright colors.

"Jim Joneses?" I asked, taking the nearest half-empty glass, to match my outlook of late. The liquid's shade of bright green was reminiscent of a lacquered Pop-Tart. I hate Pop-Tarts.

Taylor handed Trace a wineglass filled with swirling crimson. "Yeah. Liz told me it was tradition."

Trace accepted the glass with a smile and a cooed, "Thank you."

I glanced down into the emerald depths of my drink, looking for residue but finding none. Jim Joneses were this mad creation of our hostess. She came up with the notion one bored evening: Mix different flavors of Kool-Aid with premium-brand vodka or pure grain alcohol from Daddy's liquor cabinet—

more the size of a liquor armoire—and for one lucky glass/drinker, add a finely ground, random selection from Mommy's medicine cabinet. A few weeks ago, I had been the hapless winner and spent the whole evening out on their deck, my legs dangling over the side, mind paralyzed.

Which, considering all that had happened to me, might not be so bad. Yet, I grew wary. Doesn't liquor make you feel warm but just lower your body temperature? I took a tentative sip and found it too damn sweet and strong with alcohol, but without a trace of the bitterness that most pills always left behind. I figured my glass was safe.

"I hope it's not Cloz again. Kept me running to piss all night." Leather gloves covered Kim's hands. I watched her fingers brush against Taylor's as she accepted a glass.

Maggie said with a sneer, "You couldn't run. We had to walk you there or else risk a puddle."

Above me, Trace settled back in her chair, one hand leisurely holding the glass, the other tapping the rattan legs of a stool that Taylor sat on beside her. He raised his own glass to her in a mock toast.

First points of the evening: Taylor. "So what's the agenda?"

Liz answered me with two words. "The board."

"Do we have to, Liz?" Kim whined. "Ouija's so amputee. Can't we just pretend to have fun?" She sat down opposite the new guy.

For once, I agreed with Kim, but not for any of the same reasons. Even just pretending to contact the dead made my flesh crawl.

Our hostess seemed adamant, though. "Don't make me think you're a hundred-percent bitch. My house, my rules, remember?"

"Fine." Kim picked herself up. "I'm going outside for a smoke." She looked directly at Taylor. "Anyone want to join me?"

No one answered and she stomped her Doc Martens as she left.

Maggie brought out a box from underneath a small side table. I remember the first time I saw Liz's Ouija; I had coughed out half my Jim Jones while laughing. The designer must have been on serious drugs to draw on the lid smiling kids sitting around a table anxious to use the board. Now, the "Mystifying Oracle"—written in old, curving font on the board—scared me. The background's yellow parchment looked like jaundiced skin. A deep scratch scarred the cardboard and marred "No," as if to emphasize the word. I considered the Ouija mocking, yet dangerous, like a cyanide tablet with a cheerful candy coating.

I caught Trace's eye and shared my concern with her with a look.

"Liz, maybe this isn't such a good idea," she said, coming to my aid.

"Aww, could be fun," Taylor offered.

Maggie tossed the white plastic planchette onto the board. It landed upside down, *Made in Korea* clearly visible. "I'll protect everyone from the ghosties."

I finished off my first glass of Jim Jones in one deep gulp, anxious to pass out before something bad happened.

"So who should we try to contact?"

"How 'bout the guy on Rt. 47?" Maggie suggested.

Trace and I both shouted out "No!" Everyone looked at us.

"I know who." Taylor said softly. "Back at the Juvenile Hall, there was this guy who had the freakiest tattoo on his shoulder. More than a sketch. It looked so perfect. Creeped me out every time I saw it. So everyone asks Don—that's the guy's name—who she was.

"Don said his little sister was raped and killed by a friend of his. Don was at Burlington for beating the shit out of the guy who did it. The tattoo was so he'd never forget her."

All of us remained quiet a moment after he finished.

"Damn," muttered Maggie.

"So what do you think?"

To me it sounded like the worst idea ever. I had wanted to escape ghosts for the night, not invite one over.

But Liz and Maggie were all for it. They arranged the board between them. "You have to lead, Taylor," Liz said and waved for him to join them on the floor.

He did and looked up at Trace and smiled. She slid off her seat and sat opposite him.

"Move closer," Maggie told me.

"I'll just watch from here." I brought up my knees to my chin and wrapped my arms around my legs. Maybe nothing would happen. Not everyone who dies leaves a ghost behind. Still, I promised myself I'd stay quiet once they began. No need to attract attention.

They all put their fingers onto the planchette. Trace giggled and Liz shushed her.

"I think her name was Samantha," Taylor said. "Samantha Divvens."

For the next ten minutes they all took turns calling out to her, asking her spirit to talk to them, all the while moving the piece over the board.

But I heard Samantha first. Thumps and creaks coming from upstairs. I looked up at the stucco ceiling. The creaking of a bed? The sounds became louder.

"What was that?"

The bulb in the nearest lamp in the room popped and blew. Everyone jumped a little. Then all the lights in the house went out. Everything was dark.

"Shit," cried out Liz.

I heard Taylor say "Must have blown a circuit." I knew he was wrong.

"Trace," I whispered. "She's here."

"Where's a flashlight, hon? Or candles?" Maggie's voice remained steady.

"In the kitchen." More thuds from above. "Tell me that's Kim playing with us."

"Maybe." A hand on my shoulder startled me. "Shh, it's me," Trace said. Her voice was slightly slurred.

I heard the sound of drawers in the next room being opened and rooted through. A dim beam of light flashed in our direction. Maggie cursed. "Batteries are dying." She walked into the room, moving the light over each of us. I saw Trace leaning against Taylor, his arm around her.

Liz finished off her own drink and reached for the next nearest glass that still had some Jim Jones left. "Kim," she yelled at the ceiling, "if that's you stop fucking around!"

The thumping did not stop.

Maggie moved over to stand next to her girlfriend. "Hon, we need to find the circuit breaker."

"What is going on up there?" Taylor asked. He went over to the front windows and pulled aside the thick, velvet curtains. "Damn. The rest of the street has power."

"I don't know!" Liz wiped her mouth with the back of her hand. "Maybe the basement."

"Let's go down there. Sometimes all you need is to flip a switch or something."

"She must be pissed off," Trace muttered. She sounded very drunk. Or wasted. She even stumbled heading toward the stairs. Her glass must have been the lucky one. "I want to see her." She tottered putting one foot on the bottom step and her fingers on the banister.

They still think it's a game.

Taylor reached her before I could. "Not alone you don't." He steadied her against him.

"We should just stay here," I said in a low voice. I didn't want *her* to hear me.

"Silly boy," Trace giggled and started up with Taylor right behind. He held up a Zippo lighter, the tiny flame shedding a very weak, disheartening light.

I looked over my shoulder. Liz and Maggie were gone. No sign of Kim. I didn't want to stay in the dark by myself. Against my better judgment, I climbed the stairs after them.

The staircase curved around to the second floor landing. A hallway of doors faced us. The creaks and thuds came from down there.

"Samantha," called out Trace. I wanted to put a hand over her mouth even though I knew the ghost couldn't hear her anyway.

The first door turned out to be the bathroom. I caught a glimpse of us reflected in the mirror. I think my eyes looked wild.

The next door was ajar. Just as Trace was pushing it open, Taylor cursed and the lighter went out. "Burned my finger," he said.

Enough light came through the window to reveal a child's bedroom. The sounds suddenly died away. On the bed, lying on a colored quilt muted by moonlight, was a little girl. Her arms lay at her sides, her legs spread apart. Pretty blond hair around her head like a halo. She wore a ripped nightgown pushed up past her knees.

I took a step closer. My foot creaked on the floorboards. I looked down at a discarded doll inches away. It wore a frilly dress and a cloth cap. The turn of the doll's head gave the impression its neck was broken.

From behind me I heard a distant Trace calling out again, "Samantha." I turned around to see the door shut.

> "Baby, baby, bye,
> Close your little eye!"

The soft voice, distinctively that of a young girl singing, chilled me to the bone. I spun about but the figure on the bed remained deathly still.

> *"When the dark begins to creep*
> *Tiny-wees must go to sleep."*

The doll's mouth opened and closed in time with each verse.

> *"Lammy, lammy, lie,*
> *I am seven, I."*

I backed away until I hit the door. My hand found the knob but it would not turn.

> *"Little boys must sleep and wait*
> *If they want their bed-time late."*

I kicked back with my foot against the door. My heart raced, but I could not look away from the doll. One of its tiny plastic arms began to move back and forth, pawing at the air.

"Trace!" I screamed. "Trace!"

The doll's eyelids flicked open. It stared directly at me.

> *"Fidgy, fidgy, fie,*
> *There's no need to cry!*
> *Soon you'll never dress in white,*
> *Never sleep, though it's always night."*

The girl on the bed sat up. I could see the marks on her neck, dark traces against china-white skin where hands had choked her. "No more, Donnie. Please, no more." Her voice sounded exactly like the doll's.

The door behind me suddenly opened and I fell backward, hitting the carpeted floor of the hallway. Above me I could see Taylor and Trace's face in the welcome glow of the lighter. Both looked concerned.

"What the hell happened to you?" Taylor asked.

I rose up on my elbows. The room I had just been in looked utterly different. I faced a home office. "I don't know."

Taylor offered me a hand up. "Whatever made the sounds stopped, I think it must have been a tree branch hitting the roof."

He glanced back down the hallway. "The rest of the rooms are empty."

"No Samantha." Trace sighed. She looked half-asleep.

There was no point in telling a somnambulistic Trace that I had seen Samantha. I closed the door to the office and rested my hand against the wood. The last thing she said was far more frightening than the doll's song. I didn't think that a friend had been the one who raped her. Or killed her.

The lights came back on, making us all blink and shade our eyes.

"Guess they found the problem," Taylor said.

Maybe.

Kim met us at the bottom of the steps. She stank of strong tobacco and drank straight from a bottle of dark rum. "Playing hide-and-go-seek?"

"Where's Maggie and Liz?" I asked. I hoped they had had enough play with the Ouija board for one evening.

She nodded in the direction of the kitchen. "Arguing." She rolled her eyes. "Lame." When we headed that way, she yelled out, "Do they still call it a cat fight if two dykes are going at it?"

Through the swinging door that led into the kitchen I overheard Maggie gripe, "It was just a kiss—"

"No. You're always doing that, reaching for me," complained Liz. "God, I can't turn around without you being right next to me."

We came in to find Maggie slouched against the refrigerator door, her arms crossed over her chest. "I'm your girlfriend. We're supposed to—" She stopped when she saw us. Her face was flushed.

Liz was across the room from her, dipping a baby carrot into an open jar of salad dressing. "I'm tired of being smothered. I didn't even ask you to come tonight."

Maggie flipped Liz the finger. "Fuck you, these are my friends too. Hell, I introduced you to them."

"Uhh, I see the lights are on." I stammered.

"Genius. Now I see why you don't go to school," Liz snapped.

Ouch. "Okay, guess the party's over." I turned right around and left.

Trace followed, pouting. "Aww, no."

"It's okay." I saw Taylor standing behind her. "You stay."

"Want me to drive you?" She began looking about the room. I figured she was trying to find her purse.

"You're not driving after what you drank," Taylor said. "Do you want me to drive you?"

At the door I waved aside the request. "I'll be fine." A lie. I didn't really want to go home. Josh might be waiting for me there. Might be. But I couldn't stand to watch the girls have a relationship meltdown.

When Maggie stomped by and threw on her leather jacket by the front door, I saw my chance. Before she could grab the doorknob I moved to her side with my duster in hand.

She looked up at me with red eyes. "You leaving, too?"

"Yeah."

"C'mon, I'll give you a ride." She slammed the front door behind her.

Her Jeep was parked in the driveway. She swept some magazines off the passenger seat. "Get in, it's cold out." She turned the key too hard and the engine ground. On the next attempt, the motor roared to life and she maneuvered the stick shift into gear and backed out fast without even checking to see if any cars were coming.

"Where do you live again?"

"Off of Crestview. But let's just drive around a while, 'kay?" I was in no huge rush to get back.

"Gotcha."

Maggie gripped the steering wheel hard enough to make her fingers white. She made every turn fast, squealing the tires.

"Want to talk?"

"'Bout?" She glanced at me a second then looked back at the road.

"You and Liz obviously had a fight."

"That's all we've been doing lately." She leaned her head against her left hand.

I wasn't sure what to say but my remaining quiet must have begged her to say more.

"We've barely kissed in weeks. I don't know what she even wants anymore." Maggie barked a bitter laugh. "I don't think she knows. The bit about buying that lingerie at the shop for Halloween was a line of bullshit. I thought," she wiped an eye that started tearing. "I thought that if she saw me wearing it, something elegant, she'd want to... well... we'd..."

Inwardly, I added this moment to my top-ten list of awkward situations. The last thing I should be doing was giving out relationship advice. Me, the little goth boy being stalked by a dead jock.

Both of us were silent while we drove around town. Everything was still and quiet with few other cars about. Finally, the dashboard clock approached my curfew and I asked Maggie to take me home. She nodded and in a few minutes pulled onto my street.

"I hope it works out. I mean, when I see you guys together, I think to myself, 'That's what I want.'"

As she stopped in front of my aunt's house she favored me with a faulty grin. "Thanks."

I put my hand on her shoulder and squeezed. "I should be thanking you for the ride. You want to come in? I think we still have some awful cocoa mix left over."

That made her laugh. "No, I'm thinking I might ride around a while, clear my head."

"I'm envious about the tongue piercing." Actually the truth. I stepped out onto the curb.

"Heh, the only reason I got it was 'cause I thought she'd like it." She gave me a little wave and then drove off.

I watched the lights from the Jeep get smaller and smaller until I realized how vulnerable I felt standing all by myself in front of the house. I dashed up to the porch and felt relieved only when I was through the front door.

Flicking off the light my aunt had left on for me, I headed to my bedroom when I felt a presence. The fine hairs on the back of my neck rose. In my mind's eye I could see him, standing there behind me, reaching out one hand toward me. I froze. Josh. I may have whispered his name or simply thought it. Did it matter?

"Where were you?" I never knew such a soft voice could be so accusing.

"With my friends." I whispered, afraid to wake my aunt. I refused to turn around.

His fingers chilled my shoulder, making me weak. In a rush, I remembered how he made me feel last night. Like an addict, I wanted his touch again.

"I'm your friend. You don't need anyone else." If Josh could breathe, I would have felt it softly against my cheek.

"Please. Not tonight." My voice trembled. I hated how he made me so afraid of giving in.

"You would rather be with them?"

I tried to focus on being back in the tub and worrying over whether I'd ever get warm again. It made it easier to say, "Josh, just go." I started walking away down the hall.

Up ahead, from the darkness of my room, two eyes glowed blue. "No."

He moved so quickly, stepping out before I could turn and run. Out of instinct, I lifted up a hand, to fend him off. My fingers met his chest, sinking through the letter jacket he wore.

I'm sitting on the floor of a landing. Across from me, leaning against the wallpaper, a red-haired girl twirls a curly lock in her fingers and smiles knowingly. Why it takes me a moment to recognize her, I don't know. She's infamous though. Arlene the school slut.

She leans forward and takes from my hand the half-full can of Blackdram beer I hadn't realized I was holding. She brings the metal cone top to her shiny pink lips. A slight trickle escapes while she drinks and she giggles and wipes her mouth with the back of her hand. I turn away, feeling uneasy. I can hear music playing downstairs.

"Josh." She nudges my penny loafer with her foot. "I'm wearing the school colors."

I look at her. Her fuzzy sweater is white with pale blue trim and the slim skirt just a shade darker. "No, you're not."

Again that giggle; it sets my teeth on edge like a dentist's drill.

"Yes, I am," she says softly and begins lifting up the edge of her skirt. Her eyelids lower. "Underneath."

Oh God, I think. I have to get out of there. I rise up, a bit unsteady. I must have had more than just a few sips of beer.

"Here, let me help you." She grabs hold of my hand and pulls me toward her. Before I can stop her, her lips are pressing against mine. I can smell her lipstick, taste it as she forces her tongue into my mouth. Sickly sweet and making me gag.

Bile rising, I push her off me and rush toward the first door in sight, hoping it's the bathroom. Luck's with me, and I could almost sigh in thanks to see the toilet if I wasn't nauseated.

"Josh, are you okay?" Arlene knocks on the door a few times while I'm throwing up.

After flushing, I move to the sink, turning the faucets and splashing water on my face. When I look up, I cry out. The face in the mirror. It isn't my own. Some scrawny kid with dark hair and girlish features stares out at me.

"Josh, you're scaring me."

I turn around at Arlene's shout. When I look back all I see is my dripping face, looking pale and slightly wild-eyed. Maybe the beer has skunked on me.

"It's okay," I call out to her. "I just need to be alone a moment."

She doesn't answer. I cup a handful of cool water and rinse out the bad taste in my mouth. I dry myself with one of the hand towels. Then open up the medicine cabinet. My eyes fall on the bottle of Old Spice. Gary's father's. That's right, I remember the gathering is at Gary Mitchell's house while his folks are away for the weekend.

I uncap the bottle and take a deep sniff. Such a wonderful smell. I close my eyes and think of Gary's father back at a summer barbeque, wearing a T-shirt that showed off the man's muscles and the hint of graying chest hair.

Roddy would look as good when he was forty. Roddy. I never stop thinking of him. I should be downstairs next to him, not that jerk, Colin. My only reason for being up here with Arlene was a plan to make Roddy jealous. He doesn't seem to care.

With my fingers clutching the cologne, I smash the bottle into the mirror. The act, so brief, does not help. If anything, it leaves me wound even tighter. I look down at the shards of glass in the sink. My reflection lies shattered. One blue eye stares back at me in over a dozen places.

Arlene isn't waiting for me outside the bathroom. I take the steps down two at a time. I'll talk to Roddy, get him to see what a mistake he's making, what he risks losing. Me. He should be wanting me.

Down in the rec room the Everly Brothers are singing off a 45.

Bye bye love, bye bye sweet caress,
hello emptiness
I feel like I could di-ie

"No." Josh gasped. He disappeared and a moment later re-appeared way down the hall, his gaze on the ground.

My heart raced. I sought to cling to his memories, eager to know what frightened him so, but our contact had been too brief.

"I won't lose you." Josh began to fade. "Not again."

I kept hearing those words and his voice even after he had vanished.

Chapter 8

At the shop, nothing went right. My mind wasn't on straightening up. I waited for Trace to call me; I felt sure she would. But the phone remained quiet. Finally, at around four, I couldn't stand being all alone and anxious anymore. I closed up, telling myself that no one would have come by anyway and that if Malvern found out, I'd say I didn't feel well. I hated doing it, but I couldn't stay there. I needed to do something about what had happened last night. Trace would understand.

Her car wasn't parked outside her house but Second Mike's bike leaned against the porch steps. A wonderful smell drifted from nearby, burning leaves on the breeze, my favorite scent of autumn.

I rang the doorbell. No one answered even after I pushed twice more. The windows were dark. Laughter, trailing from around back, reached me. The smell intensified as I walked around.

115

The Vaughn backyard looked like an abandoned archaeological dig. Remnants of old toys and playthings were scattered about. A battered slide. A leaking sandbox. Closer to the house, a picnic table and benches. Second Mike stood in front of the open barbeque grill his father had bought last month. In one hand he held up a clump of brown leaves. When he saw me, he smiled and dropped them onto the coals. Gray smoke rose up, tinting the air around him.

"Grab some," he called out and headed over to the nearest pile by a fallen rake.

I went over to him.

"So who'd you come over for? My sister?"

"Maybe." I reached down and grabbed a small branch. I poked him lightly in the side with it. "Maybe not." I wasn't really lying. Still, I had to wonder how I could let myself sweat Second Mike. Wasn't it wrong to be so into your best friend's little brother? But his quirkiness intrigued me, made me want to know him better.

He paused to look up at me. "Oh?"

"Where's she at anyway?"

Mike seemed disappointed that I asked. He shrugged his thin shoulders and went back to picking up more leaves. "The supermarket."

A small leaf, the edges curled, was stuck on the back of his T-shirt below the neckline. I reached for it, plucking it off. He turned around and watched as I crumpled it in my hand. "The yellow ones are especially dangerous."

He rolled his eyes but didn't laugh and left me feeling totally self-conscious. What was I doing, standing there? I realized I so wanted him to just kiss me again, yet I couldn't bring myself to make a move.

He dropped another handful into the open grill. We both watched as the leaves quickly caught fire, becoming incandescent orange before turning ash gray.

"Burning them is illegal."

"So?" He wiped his hands on his shirt.

I grinned. "Maybe I should turn you in?" I couldn't believe I was flirting or that it seemed so easy, as if instinctual.

He surprised me by suddenly lunging, pushing and knocking me over. I landed in the pile, hearing their crackle beneath me. "Arrest me then." He held out both arms to me, wrists upturned.

I paused, unsure what I should do next. Was this flirting back or just roughhousing?

I dared to reach up and grab an arm, pulling him down on top of me. He landed on my chest. His face, only inches from my own, seemed caught in a moment of delight before softening to uncertainty.

With a hand still on his arm, I could feel his pulse quickening beneath my touch. My mouth dried up as we stared at each other. I wondered what he was thinking. I would have given anything to know.

Second Mike scooted forward, sliding over me. With my other hand I reached up and brushed my fingers through his short hair, marveling at the soft texture. He allowed my fingers to roam. His lips parted slightly and his eyes closed.

I hesitated only a moment to wonder how I had ever deserved his interest. Then I rose up and kissed him, my tongue slipping effortlessly into his warm mouth. I felt more, then heard his gasp and panicked a moment, worried that I had done wrong. But he never pulled away, instead pushing himself down upon me.

We lay there together, holding each other, barely breathing as we kissed. I kept my eyes open, taking in the sight of him so close. Deliriously counting the freckles on his forehead, all seven, I was thankful I could see nothing else but him.

I never heard her footsteps; Mike had done too thorough a job of clearing the lawn of leaves. But the thud and something appearing suddenly beside my head shocked me. Mike too jumped, breaking our kiss and falling off me.

I turned and saw a very full grocery bag lying next to me. Trace stood behind it, staring down at us. Her face looked drawn.

Our words tumbled together, Mike and I both trying to explain, as we disentangled ourselves. My face burnt red. Trace bit her lip as she picked up the bag and brought it over to the picnic table. Mike looked at me nervously a moment before following after her.

"I didn't expect you. We're having a little sister-brother picnic." She lifted up a wrapped package of meat and let it drop to the table while looking right at me. "Seems you're more than welcome to stay. Why don't you go inside and get some plates?"

I opened my mouth, hoping that something brilliant would come out and explain away everything she had seen. But I only stuttered out a syllable before she said "plates" again and pointed toward the house.

I gave Second Mike a sympathetic shrug and headed for the back door. Inside, the house was dim. As I moved into the kitchen, out of the corner of my eye I saw something move. I looked around but saw nothing; the entire house seemed hushed, expectant. When I went over to the cabinets I felt watched and the muscles in my back tensed, stiffening my shoulders. I grabbed some plates and turned around and found myself face to face with Mike.

Surprised, I jumped a little, the plates rattling unsteadily in my hand. I almost relaxed, almost gave him a smile and reached out to touch him when I realized it wasn't Second Mike standing in front of me. The resemblance was uncanny; if I had been spending so much time of late paying attention to Mike's features I would never have noticed the difference. This boy's face was smaller, younger, and the hair a bit darker. He wore clothes I had seen Mike wear, but in better shape; the jeans looked almost new.

I took a step back, feeling my backbone strike the edge of the countertop. First Mike—it could only be him, his ghost—did not move. He just stared at me.

As I stood there, I could sense the sadness surrounding First Mike's spirit with an almost tangible aura. A little red bubble formed from one nostril on the slight nose. Mesmerized, I watched it grow little by little until it popped, silently. Then a rivulet of blood began, leaving a bright, crimson trail over the lips and chin. I watched the drops fall and leave little splatter marks on the linoleum. The ghost remained as motionless as a marble statue.

I ran. By the time I had reached the backyard, my mind had reached new heights of paranoia; how many times had I mistaken what-I-thought-was Second Mike in the house for his dead brother? Once or twice? Countless times? Again, I worried how long had I been seeing ghosts and not realizing it? Months?

Trace and Mike stared at me wide-eyed. I had trouble looking at Second Mike. I kept on expecting him to shift, to change into his older brother.

"I saw him," I gasped. "Inside."

"Who? Josh?" I could hear the fear in her voice.

"No. Your brother." I found myself laughing suddenly, though the joke was on me. "You always said the place was haunted. Why didn't we check it out? See who was home?"

"Calm down." Trace held my face in both her hands. "Mike, I'll be right back. Stay with him."

I watched her go in. I think I called out, "Why not invite him over? Make it a sister-brother-brother picnic." I didn't like the hysterical note in my own voice.

Mike rubbed my back and stayed close. I closed my eyes and the plates I held slipped and would have fallen if Mike hadn't caught them.

"Sorry," I said, embarrassed at him seeing me like that. My sense of shame seemed to calm me down.

"Would have been easy to clean up."

"No, for freaking out like this." I sat down on the bench. What was taking Trace so long?

He remained quiet a moment. "Did you really see him?"

I nodded.

"What was he like?" He sat on the table top facing me.

This had to be rough on him, also. I wanted to shield him, keep him safe and unaware of such things as ghosts. "You're cuter," I said, weakly trying to make light of the situation. He blushed.

Trace came back out then. "Nothing in there."

"Was there any blood on the floor?"

She hadn't expected that question. "Not a drop."

I rubbed my face, feeling unsteady. "He was there."

"So he really is dead." She stared at the house. "I guess we all knew, but no one liked to talk about it." She reached for her purse. Her hand shook. "Mike, mind getting the bottle that's in the trunk?" She tossed him the keys. He caught them and nodded.

"Are you okay?" I asked as Mike dashed off around front.

"No. I—I don't know what to think. I want an explanation of what I saw."

"Maybe we can help him—"

She held up a hand, stopping me. "No, that bit with you and Second Mike. Not right now. I don't want him to come back to an argument. Just think about it."

An apology came to my lips too late. I should never have hidden something so sensitive from her. Out of the corner of my eye, I caught Mike returning with the liquor bottle.

"Remember," she said to me softly. "He means more to me than any friendship." She smiled at Mike when he handed her the half empty bottle of gin. "I know I need a drink."

I was more numb than tipsy when I left them. It had been an awkward picnic. I didn't know who or where to look. If my eyes spent too much time lingering on Mike, I felt caught in the act of further wrongdoing. If I looked at Trace, I could see the disappointment and worry in her own eyes. Even the house seemed threatening to gaze at. So I kept quiet mostly, pushing the food around on my plate, until the sky had darkened. My goodbye to both seemed measly; I knew I should have done more: at least a hug with Mike and just finding the right words to say to Trace. But I couldn't; I felt helpless.

On the walk home, I kept thinking how sad his spirit was. Are all ghosts miserable in their undeath? Never knowing peace, always lurking about, often unseen and unheard, year after year? Did Josh want me not out of love but more out of a desperate need to keep from being lonely? I remembered that fear.

If only there was some way to free them. Maybe a séance was necessary. If I managed to talk to First Mike's ghost, find out why he haunted the house, that might be the first step.

At home, I dialed the only person I knew who owned a Ouija board.

Liz picked up the phone on the third ring. "You're not still angry, are you? Or are we going to have to play Sorry for a while?"

Inwardly I groaned. It was never wise to come near either Liz or Maggie when they were fighting. "Liz, it's me."

She quickly recovered from her surprise. "This is a first. You've never called me before."

"Yeah, sorry 'bout that. Listen, can I stop by and borrow that Ouija board?"

"Now's not so good—"

"C'mon, I'm desperate."

No sound from the other end and for a moment I worried that somehow I lost her. "Why do you need the board?"

What could I say that didn't sound insane? But then, this was Liz, the girl who liked to dope her guests, who once thought that a mix of self-hypnosis tapes and masturbation would lead to a better O.

"If I'm lucky, I'll speak to a ghost."

Liz chuckled. I breathed easier. "Anyone I know?"

"Trace's older brother." I regretted saying it instantly. My insanity was one thing, but revealing Trace's involvement in even a distant way was wrong.

"Oh." Again some silence. "What are you wearing?"

"What was that?"

"How are you dressed? Old clothes or new?"

"Umm, new. Black T-shirt and dyed-red jeans."

"Hmmm, okay. Come over."

I hung up feeling as confused as if I had drunk three of those damn Jim Joneses.

Liz answered the door with an awkward smile. For once she looked sedate, no wild colors in her hair, on her face, or in her clothes. She wore a simple dress, ivory with black Chinese script running from the left shoulder to her leg. Her "pagoda outfit" I think she had once called it. She stepped outside, blocking my way into the house.

"Before we go in, let me say two things. One, I'm sorry to have to do this to you, and two, thanks for being a great friend." Then she took my hand and pulled me in. I had no time to wonder at anything she said.

"Here he is," she called out playfully and tugged me into the living room.

I found myself facing a stylish pair of adults. Her folks? They smiled at me and instinctively I smiled back. "Uhhh…" I began.

Liz wrapped her arms around me and gave me a hug. Waves of "wrong" swept through me. "Isn't he cute?" she cooed. I didn't think girls still cooed.

Her mother, dressed all designerish, stood up. "Oh yes." She sized me up and down like something at the butcher's. My blush deepened—if I had been lucky, I would have passed out from the blood rushing to my head.

Liz's father stepped over and held out his hand. He wore a sweater and sport jacket that probably cost as much as my favorites at Malvern's. "Ashby," he said, "we've heard a lot about you."

Ashby?

Liz kissed my ear and at the same time whispered there, "Play along, please."

I took her father's hand. "Thanks. I can only imagine what she's told you."

"Well, she did say you were taller." He laughed suddenly and I realized it was a joke. "Heh." My forced smile ached.

"I'm going to take Ashby into the kitchen for something to drink." She pulled me through the swinging door.

"What have you done to me?" I hissed once we were hidden away from her parents. "Ashby?"

She put her finger over my lips, which made me pull back at the intimate touch. "Shhh, I had to do this. They think I'm dating."

"Breaking news, but you are."

"Don't be such a bitch." She glanced back in the direction of the living room, but we were safe behind the swinging door. "They can't find out about her. Look what happened to you."

Oh, she was evil, playing the trump card she knew I could not refuse. "Okay, okay, I'll play. But only for a little while. And I still need the Ouija."

She opened the fridge and pulled out a fat glass pitcher filled with red liquid and tranquil, floating orange slices. I prayed for sangria but after a sip my tongue cringed at the overripe sweetness. Just fruit punch.

"And Ashby's a cute name for a boy. It's very pretty."

"Very glam." Frustrated that my plans might have to be put off for another night, I took another sip. Maybe I'd go into a diabetic coma and could avoid the ruse.

No such luck, though. I followed Liz back out.

Hours later and we were having after-dinner drinks— alcohol for her parents, tame stuff for Liz and me—at this coffeehouse/bar, Cosi, in Philadelphia. Actually, I found out there's a chain of them around the city and I'm sure elsewhere. Not on par with DeBevec's, but the curved lines in the furnishings and funky, decorated walls, plus a pretentious menu, had the place growing on me with each passing moment.

Liz sat uncomfortably snug against me on a padded bench. Her perfume had been rather nice at the start but by dessert time I had been overexposed. Across the tiny table, her folks relaxed in overstuffed chairs.

I sipped my raspberry yogurt shake—an impulse choice— and enviously eyed Mr. Liz's mocha vodka martini garnished by a chocolate-covered espresso bean for a touch of whimsy. "Thanks for dinner. You shouldn't have."

As much as I enjoyed eating at a ritzy restaurant where presentation on the plate becomes as important as the taste of the food, it had been an awkward meal. Awkward, hell, it had been torture, fielding questions, always feeling one step slower than when Liz answered them. Plus I felt betrayed by the eyes of a cute blond waiter who made me regret holding Liz's hand so often.

I glanced back to the menu of drinks and fare on the far wall above the counter, alert to all the concoctions made with mint. My mind drifted back to the wonderful taste of Mike's mouth back in the shop.

"Daddy, Ashby and I want to stay a while in the city." Though she had finished off her hot chocolate fifteen minutes ago, she still held the mug in both hands.

Her father tilted back his martini, finishing off the muddy drink. He left the garnish to sit, lonesome, at the bottom of the glass. I heard him say something but I fixated on the bean. I wondered if, while still damp, the taste would be some wondrous mixture of bitter coffee, chocolate, and alcohol or just cloying on the tongue. Liz squeezed my arm, bringing my attention back to the conversation.

Mrs. Liz patted her husband's knee, a gesture that seemed more quaint than affectionate. "Charles, let them. They can take a cab back."

"All right then." He opened his wallet and handed her some folded bills. "Here's some spending money."

"Thanks." She cooed some more. I glanced back at the bean. Did the servers ever pop the unwanted beans into their mouth in private after taking away the glasses?

We waved goodbye to her folks and started walking down the block. Once they were out of sight, I dropped her hand. "Great. What an evening." I rubbed the back of my neck, feeling the tension under my skin like a new bone. "Please tell me that I made a good beard."

"You were the perfect date." Liz checked her watch. "Weird thing is, I think they like you."

"Great. I missed my calling as a straight man. So now what?"

"Well, tomorrow they'll be off, to Atlantic City or New York or something, leaving me alone again." She brought her hands together in mock prayer and gazed impiously downward at the pavement. "You can come by then and get the board."

"So tonight—"

"Tonight, I'm going to Sisters. Fuck Maggie." She reached into the small purse that dangled from her shoulder on a black link chain and pulled out a tiny tube. She snapped it in her fingers and it glowed a merry red. She popped it into her mouth. "You wanna come along, or do you need cash to get back to Jersey?"

I'll admit, having a conversation with someone whose mouth glows, even if it's a small glow that just highlighted the teeth and tongue, was damn cool. Also, I honestly I worried that Josh would be waiting for me at home. This would be safer for a while. "I'm game." I felt sorry, though, for Maggie. I almost asked Liz what her girlfriend had done to deserve being treated like shit, but I knew better than to provoke her.

"Do you have a spare one of those?" While fascinated by the glow, I did remember I should at least call my aunt. Letting her know I'd be out late might keep away another lecture. "You have a cell phone, right?"

She smirked. "All spoiled girls do." She went into the purse again and brought out a slender gunmetal gray phone so compact and ugly looking, it surprised me that it belonged to her. "And you're in luck, if you don't mind blue." She lifted another light tube.

I grinned, all excited, and opened my mouth. She giggled, the first honest bout from her the whole evening, and snapped it before popping it onto my tongue. "There. Are we friends now?"

"Mmmm hmmm." I nodded, feeling the strange sensation of the little plastic tube rolling around my mouth. A bland, rather disappointing taste, so I closed my eyes to better imagine how a blue glow should taste. At the very least, I knew my mouth looked odd.

She pressed the phone into my hand. "C'mon."

As I dialed, I walked behind her. She led us through the streets of Center City. The night air was pleasant, with a touch of warmth from summer months long past, and others were out roaming, mostly in pairs and groups.

The answering machine picked up. While I hated talking to a machine, good judgment finally won over with the beep. I dashed off a few slightly garbled words letting my aunt know I was alive and well in Philadelphia. Hopefully, talking with the glow stick in my mouth didn't make me sound drunk.

Liz had stopped at the corner of 13th and Locust Street. Her body language read relaxed with a capital R. "So, is it safe for you to play?"

I nodded. I told myself that I'd make it home by curfew. Maybe.

"Neat," was all she said to that.

People our age walked the street, dressed either trendy gay or preppy gay. I was a wholly different species that seemed to have no natural place in the local environment. Goth gay. When one or two of the boys looked at me, I became uncomfortable, nervous, and curious all at once. What did they think of me? I worried that I seemed so dissimilar that they'd reject me. Maybe hate me. I clung to Liz's side.

We turned down a dreary-looking side street and headed toward the double doors beneath an awning. A unique pair guarded the entrance: a thick-set woman wearing a cardigan sweater and slacks who had foolishly opted to make her face look rounder than necessary with a short haircut and large spectacles; next to her stood a girl a couple years older than Liz, maybe, but with less taste in clothing. I felt sorry for her, wearing her jean overalls, tan boots, and long braids. Almost a construction-worker wannabe chatting up a professor.

The chalkboard sign beside the doorway read *Schoolgirl Nite, No ID = No Drinks, $10 Cover* in thickly drawn rainbow letters. The two smiled at us as the older woman held open the door. Liz gave her a peppy "thanks."

While I stood shocked at the sheer number of laughing, drinking, smoking women wrapped around the bar, Liz paid for our entry. I meekly lifted up my hand for the stamp, then laughed at what I saw garnishing my wrist. A pink Venus symbol.

Liz led me through Sisters. Most of the women were much older than us, in their mid-thirties and forties. Every one of them seemed to have either a cigarette or a drink in their hands, sometimes both, sometimes taking one from the woman beside them.

Even the stairs leading up to the next floor were crowded, though the women were getting younger and younger as we climbed. The walls and steps reverberated with the beat above. The second level held the dance floor and another, smaller bar. Everywhere lights flashed. An old strobe machine threw out a flare from the ceiling with far less regularity than it had in its youth. The mirrored walls reflected all the gyrating bodies, the swinging hair and limbs. Many of the girls smiled and leered and laughed at one another with mouths that held tiny neon glows in every color imaginable.

Liz grabbed my arm and pulled me along as she threaded her way through the crowd until we were well into the midst of the throng. "Don't dance all mopey for once." Liz yelled at me. I could barely hear her over the music. She already swayed to one side and then the other, her eyes closed, mouth slightly open.

I went and bought the most expensive Coke ever at the bar. When I looked back for Liz, her spot on the dance floor had been taken by other girls. A moment's panic filled me; where was my guide that night? Had I been left stranded in the middle of a girl-on-girl storm? I pushed my way through the mass to reach the bar and found it practically deserted. Everyone was dancing or at the fringes of the room talking, laughing, kissing, petting.

The ice in my soda had melted down to slivers when Liz tapped me on the back. She was all cheery and held up a little bit of folded paper. "I have more to share tonight." Already drunk and stumbling, she leaned close to me. The blue stains at the corners of her mouth came from the shots they offered in tiny test tubes on the club floor.

She carefully unfolded the paper, which turned out to be cut from some comic strip. Two little white pills rested near a depiction of a cartoon cat fishing.

"Sweet E, sweetie, sweet E." She giggled at her silly word-play and almost dropped what I gathered was Ecstasy. That only made her laugh more.

I picked up one of the pills. I had never taken a hit of E before. I rolled it lightly between my fingers. How would the chemicals locked inside affect me? Were goths ever allowed to be euphoric?

"Go on, hon." Liz stole my drink and tipped the glass back to wash the tablet down.

I closed my eyes and dropped it onto my tongue, next to the glow stick. Liz handed my cup back to me, but when I opened my eyes I saw it was actually a new one, filled not with soda but cranberry juice and probably more. I took a sip and let the pill slip down my throat.

"Finish that and let's dance some more."

I took a few healthy swallows. On the last one, Liz tipped the bottom up, forcing me to drink the rest down all at once. She giggled and I copied her, feeling less out of place, and, dare I admit, relaxed. I drifted back onto the dance floor with her.

Someone pulled at my belt loop. I turned to find a bleached-blonde girl grinning at me. She wore a blue vest made of satin with a matching bow tie. She hooked her fingers in my jeans and pulled me tight against her. I think she realized how shocked, almost scared I was, because her smile turned gentle. "I like your blue," she said into my ear, loud enough for me to hear above the dance beat. "Let me borrow it."

She put her lips against mine and used her tongue to pry open my mouth. I fought the odd intrusion for a moment, and then gave in. Surrounded by wildness, my mind wandering, I let myself be drawn into the fold. Her tongue in my mouth seeking the glow tube seemed exciting and perverse at the same time. Somewhere in my mind whispered a voice, telling me I was deep kissing a girl and that it was definitely wrong. Was it fair I wasn't with Mike? But it was a tiny voice, barely heard over the music, barely noticed because I focused on the wickedly fun task of pushing the glow stick in her mouth and then pulling it back to mine again and again. I realized I was grinning while we kissed. But she played the game better than me and gained her prize. The kiss lingered a moment longer then, maybe as an expression of the intoxicated joy she wanted to share with me. Maybe. Then the girl who liked blue let go of me, winked, and flaunted her new cerulean smile. I watched her go, wondering if this was her fix, if on some other night, she prowled for other colors.

After that, I could only remember a few things. Liz waylaid the girl who walked through the club floor bearing a rack of test tube shots and bought a handful for each of us. She danced with several girls, laughing, hugging them in the midst of swirling figures. Liz smirked at me with blue-stained lips, her breath smelling like Curaçao. The Blue Girl came back and held Liz's face in her hands and tried to lick the color from her mouth.

I reached terminal light-headedness and left the dance floor, went over to the mirrored walls and leaned back, counting to ten and catching a breath. They both found me so many minutes later. Liz leaned her head against the Blue Girl and nibbled on her chain of azure beads.

"We're going back to my place." Blue Girl reached out to lay cool fingers on my neck. They tickled me. "Why don't you come along?"

The offer tempted me, mostly because I was curious with the need to see if the girl changed her apartment's decor with every new color fad. Would I sink into a bed with pillows the color of berries and beach glass and raw cobalt? My mind loitered there a while before I realized who I'd be sharing that bed with. That registered as wrong, though through the haze of modern pharmaceuticals I wasn't utterly sure why.

"Nah, I'm totally drawn." I held out a hand. "Can I have some cash for a ride back?"

Liz held out her purse to me. I unsnapped it and rooted around to find two twenties. I kissed both girls goodbye too many times.

A bartender called me a cab, I think. Crossing the bridge back into New Jersey, I stared at all the lights lost in the glow. As we pulled up to the driveway of my aunt's I found myself wiped and dragging and almost forgot to pay the driver. I don't even remember going inside.

Chapter 9

It was early and I sat at the kitchen table sipping tonic water and Clamato juice. My aunt insisted it's a remedy for a hangover. I thought it scary she even kept such a thing in the fridge. My temples still ached something fierce even after half a glass. When the doorbell rang it echoed in my head. I think Aunt Jan was torturing me for being late for curfew. I could not decide what was worse about the drink: the sweet quinine, keeping me from catching malaria in New Jersey, or the fact I was drinking sour runoff from a shellfish?

Maggie followed my aunt into the room. My friend looked pale, washed out, her hoodie sweatshirt with its *What Girls Like* emblem and home-cut jean shorts dingy. I groaned, suddenly sure that later on Aunt Jan would be asking *questions* about Maggie.

"Here he is," Aunt Jan said, her arms crossing over her chest. "I don't think he's moved in the past hour since I woke him."

I lifted a hand to Maggie and gave a half-hearted wave.

"You're alive after all," muttered my aunt. Turning to Maggie, she asked, "Do you want anything to drink?"

"No, thanks."

"Fine, then. *I'm* going back to bed. Last night it was so cold in this house I had to turn the heat on. I barely slept."

Maggie pulled out a chair and sat down across from me.

"Why are you here?" I garbled out. "Sane people sleep in on weekends." I wondered which of our eyes looked more bloodshot.

"I was looking for Trace."

"Her house might be a good idea." I tipped my head back and drank the rest in one foul swallow. Afterwards, I regretted not dumping it down the drain.

"Already did. I can't find Liz. Been calling everyone and no one's around." She tapped the silver rings on her fingers against the mouth of the Clamato jar. "Thought she might be here."

Shit, I suddenly remembered not only where Liz was but with whom. The Blue Girl.

Maggie must have seen the look on my face and confused it for hurt. "Not that you're last on the list." She grew agitated. "I just know something's wrong. Liz's not answering her cell phone and when I called her house her freakin' asshole parents told me—"

I closed my eyes dreading what was to come next.

"—that she wasn't home, that she was still in Philly with her *boyfriend*!" She slapped the table, startling me. "What the fuck does that mean?"

"Shh, aunt, remember?" Lesbian drama was as much a cure for a hangover as clam-flavored tomato juice.

"Sorry." She hunched her shoulders up defensively.

"Ashby." My mouth tasted awful, acrid like blood.

"What?"

"Ashby. I'm…" I rubbed my face a moment, trying to organize my thoughts. "No, he's her boyfriend. Not really. At least they think he is."

She leaned in close. "You don't want to confuse me right now," she said with almost a growl.

"Okay, from the beginning." I stifled a yawn. "Last night she asked me to pretend I was her boyfriend. She told her folks she was dating a boy named Ashby."

"Fuck." She brought a hand to her face, biting down on a knuckle. "She's such a coward."

"Maybe." Not that I was defending Liz's lies but I at least understood her need to hide. "Not everyone's folks are so accepting."

"So you went into Philly with her last night?"

"Yeah." I shut my eyes momentarily, worried over how ugly this all might get. "Hung out with her folks."

"I hate her parents. Such phonies." She grabbed the Clamato bottle and glanced at the label a moment. Whatever she saw under ingredients made her grimace. "She's turning into one too."

I didn't want to be the one holding the match to the powder keg that was Maggie and Liz's relationship. I wished I had never gone out last night. "Listen, let's take a drive. I need a favor and we can talk."

As I threw on fresh clothes and brushed my teeth, I struggled over what to tell her. If I kept dumb and silent then I really was siding with Liz. Someday, somehow, Maggie might find out about the Blue Girl. Then she'd figure out I had lied to her by omission. But telling her outright would hurt her too.

"Where to?" Maggie asked, putting a hand on the gearshift.

"The Soulless Megastore."

"Ah." She had briefly worked at the Soulless Megastore for a few weeks until she decided to get her septum pierced. Her weasel of a manager told her to take it out or leave. Maggie made sure everyone in the store knew she walked out. The ironic thing was, two weeks later she had the ring removed because it kept irritating her nose and making it bleed.

By the time I climbed into Maggie's Jeep, I decided to tell her everything. Maggie deserved the truth. She had always been up front with me. Plus, she had come to my rescue back at the drive-in. If they did break up, it wouldn't be my fault, not really. Liz had done the cheating.

"We went to Sisters last night," I began.

I saw how she stiffened behind the wheel. "Really." The Jeep started to gain speed.

I had gone to enough drivers' ed classes to know you shouldn't drive angry—maybe I should have waited until we reached the Megastore. "Yeah. Somehow we both got in."

"And?" She clicked her tongue stud against her front lower teeth.

I squirmed in my seat a little, and then played with the automatic window. "Was crowded. Never been around that many women before." My weak joke quickly died against her silence. "Anyways. I just followed Liz's lead."

"Yeah, she goes there a lot now. Ever since she bought fake ID."

"So we had some drinks. I don't remember what they were called. Then she gave me some Ecstasy—"

"Bitch." Maggie snarled and smacked the steering wheel. "Whenever she rolls, she gets bad."

"There's more. It gets worse."

She nodded. "Tell me," she muttered with a clenched jaw.

"She was dancing with this girl. They kissed too. I... I took a cab home. By myself." I put a hand on her shoulder and squeezed. "I'm sorry. I'm sorry that it happened." I felt so awful telling her all this. Maggie remained still, like a statue.

We pulled into the parking lot, narrowly missing a vagrant shopping cart. Maggie hit it with her car door getting out and started cursing loudly. I counted at least four "fucks" and one "cunt" before she stopped.

"What are we here for anyway?"

"Umm, a Ouija set. I had gone over to... well, her house to pick it up when I got dragged into the mess."

She gave me a nasty look as we walked through the mechanical doors.

I preferred the flea market to the Megastore. The fluorescent overhead bulbs cast everything and everyone in a stark, unflattering light. The air was cool, recycled endlessly until it had a weird taint to it. Garish signs promising the lowest prices on crap no one needed, let alone wanted, distracted me.

Maggie headed right for the candy aisle. I guess she needed the comfort of sugar. She didn't seem to even hear me when I called out I'd be by the toys.

Little kids ran amuck around me, screaming and tossing gigantic plastic balls at one another as I searched the shelves. *Bash! Go for Broke. Last Straw. Steeplechase.* I saw one dusty box with a haunted house on it. *Which Witch?* Trace would have laughed at the grinning cartoon witches on the cover. Maybe it would make a nice peace offering? I needed to make amends for betraying her trust.

I couldn't find any Ouija boards. I wanted to bang my sore forehead against the metal shelves. Another delay as I'd have to look elsewhere. Was fate trying to tell me another séance was a bad idea?

I found Maggie leaning against a rack of confectionaries. She cried while she peeled away a candy bar's wrapper and took a bite. Her fingertips smeared with melted chocolate and sticky caramel. She sobbed and dropped the bar onto the floor with the others, sampled and discarded.

"Maggie, we should go." When I reached for her, she stepped back.

"Why are there no Valomilks?" She tugged at the display shelf, knocking more of the sweets off. "What kind of store doesn't sell Valomilks? They're my favorite."

A middle-aged man, small with large glasses and badly parted hair, came over to us. He wore the traditional Megastore vest over a cheap button-down shirt.

"Uhh, do you need some help?"

Maggie nodded and wiped at her eyes, leaving a brown smear on her forehead and cheek. She walked over to him, kicking aside some of the fallen candy. "Do you have a girl-friend?"

He blinked a few times, eyes greatly magnified behind the glass, then replied with a meek, "No."

"Good." She reached out to adjust his polyester vest. "'Cause all women are fucking whores!"

The poor guy backpedaled, then ran from us.

Laughing, Maggie nearly doubled over. Yet she still cried. I gently took hold of her by the shoulders. "Let's get out of here."

She glanced down at the box of *Which Witch?* I carried. "You didn't get a Ouija."

"Not a one in the place. I'll have to go to the mall or some-thing."

As we walked over to the checkout, Maggie stopped me, grabbing an arm. I turned around and saw her reaching into a display of discounted mouse pads. "Thought I saw… " She pushed the topmost ones so they slid off into the aisle. "Yes." She held up a pad decorated to resemble a Ouija board. "Two-twenty-nine."

I hugged her tight, smelling chocolate and nougat on her skin. "You're the best."

Her head nestled in the crook of my neck, she whispered back, "Why doesn't she think that?"

"I don't know." She looked at me with such sad eyes, I had to say something else to comfort her. "Maybe, because we start with people that aren't right for us. We're so busy wanting love that we never even think what the hell love needs back. I mean, you find a sexy guy… or girl," I said squeezing her once, "and she's all hot for you but there has to be more to it than that."

"You're getting all philosophical in the middle of the Megastore. That's freakish." Maggie shook her head and laughed.

I was planning out in my head how I'd be contacting First Mike and what I'd be asking his spirit, when I noticed that Maggie wasn't heading back to my aunt's house. Instead she turned onto the interstate highway and began driving north.

"I need to get out of this fucking town for a lil' while," she said.

I nodded and fiddled with the radio, finding a college station that played a song by the Redcaps we both liked.

Thirty minutes later we pulled over on the shoulder of a small road by the Delaware Canal. Leaves in vibrant shades of rust and amber and maroon rustled on the trees and drifted down on the breeze. A fat, coppery oak leaf fell on Maggie's head as she left the car and headed down to paved path alongside the water's edge.

I followed and sat down next to her on the bank of the canal. The air smelled so crisp I thought it might snap when I took a breath.

"You're right, you know," Maggie said, pitching a twig into the slow current.

"Oh?"

"Love's so *hard*." Maggie paused to wipe at the fresh tears that ran down her face. "I met Liz freshman year. She caught me staring at her in the girl's locker room. I blushed. She smiled. I thought that was that. Only, after class a few days later she pulled me aside, asked me to come over. This pretty girl wanting to hang with me." Maggie shook her head. "That house. Like a mansion to me. We spent the afternoon laughing on her bed, listening to Ani DiFranco, and drinking liquor she snuck from her dad's cabinet. She was all I thought about for days, no, weeks, afterwards.

"I never dared asked myself why she wanted to be with me."

I leaned my chin on her head, tickling my face with her gel-stiffened hair. "I bet you were her first girl, too."

"So was that the reason? We were the only lezzies in school so we drifted together?" She picked up a nearby acorn.

"Maybe. But if Liz doesn't care for who you really are inside, there are girls out there that will. Trust me." It felt weird offering advice on love. Would I really be saying all this if it weren't for Josh and Mike, finally understanding how easy it was to fall for the wrong person while the right one is underfoot?

"I need a drink," she muttered and tossed the nut into the canal.

"Ugh," I said, still not fully recovered from the night before. "I've had enough alcohol to last the year. How about ice cream instead? Remember the place in New Hope? 'Bout fifteen minutes from here."

"Much better."

I think I saw a hint of a smile on her face.

We walked around scenic New Hope, a small town that catered to motorcycle gangs and thick-walleted tourists. Often leaning against each other, not so much for support but just to get that physical sense needed for friendship, we ate our cones of cinnamon and pumpkin. I didn't mention Liz or thoughts on love being a chore. Maggie distracted herself with admiring the Harleys lined up in front of the local biker hangout and checking out the fetish wear at the corset shop. We ate dinner we could barely afford at this little bistro on the river, tossing bits of French bread to hungry ducks. I told myself one day I'd bring Mike out there, sure he would enjoy it. He'd probably start rambling about local history and I'd have to stop him with a kiss. I hid most of the smile thoughts of him brought; I did not want to burden Maggie.

It was well after dark by the time we came back to town. I asked her to drop me off at Malvern's. The Ouija pad rested in my lap.

"Do you want me to come in with you?" She stopped right outside the shop and put the Jeep's gear in park.

"No, it's okay." Part of me wanted her by my side if I did succeed in reaching First Mike's spirit, but after all she had been through, dealing with ghosts seemed like the last thing she needed.

"I don't like you playing around with this all by yourself."

"It's harmless, remember?" I hated lying to her.

"What are you going to use as a planchette?"

"Shit." I had totally forgotten about needing that. I must be the dumbest medium on the planet.

"Here," Maggie said and began lifting off her pride necklace of rainbow metal links. She handed it over and then pulled off the most ornate of the silver rings she wore. "You can hang the ring from the chain and use it as a pendulum over the board, err pad."

"Thanks." I leaned over and gave her a peck on the forehead. "You'll be okay." I hoped I sounded confident.

She nodded. "Keep the ring," she called out to me as I got out of the car. "It was a Valentine's gift." Then she sped off.

I turned the key in the shop's door and let myself inside. I didn't dare turn on the downstairs light. It would attract attention being the only lit storefront on the block.

For a moment, as I passed by the Fuji phone, I contemplated calling Trace. After all, this involved her brother, wouldn't she be further pissed off by me excluding her? But I decided against it. Suppose I failed to reach him or we couldn't help him; it would only be cruel with her emotions. I had fumbled too many encounters with ghosts to risk hurting someone else.

I shuffled my way through the dark until I reached the steps. The third floor didn't have windows and I told myself that would be the safest place to hold a séance. I waved my hand about looking for the string attached to the overhead bulb. For a moment, my imagination went wild and I had the sudden terror that when I pulled it I'd find Josh standing in a corner of the room, staring at me. I hesitated before tugging on the cord. The overhead light went on with a flicker. I was alone.

I slid two cardboard boxes together, one to sit on, one for a makeshift table. I placed the Ouija mouse pad on the box and tried not to laugh at how silly it looked. My hands shook a little as I strung the ring through the necklace and let it hang over the makeshift board. I sat down, closed my eyes, and calmed myself.

I needed to figure things out. Mostly, what the hell I could do. Deep down, I knew there was more to being a medium than seeing and talking with ghosts. Having a séance to reach First Mike would be my first experiment. Something small, something safe. Hopefully.

Though his spirit seemed to haunt only the Vaughn house, I was sure I could call him away to me, much like what happened with Samantha. I shivered at that memory. But could I get him to tell me what I wanted? Could I learn what had happened to him? More importantly, was there any way I could lay his spirit to rest?

"Mike. Mike Vaughn." I anticipated a change in the air, that same shudder inside my skin that came when I heard of some tragic accident. The barest of tremors traveled through my arm. When I opened my eyes, the ring swayed slightly, even though I was sure my hand remained steady.

"C'mon, Mike," I said under my breath. "We've met, remember? I know your family." I envisioned all the Vaughns, skipping over the father and dwelling first on Trace and then my Mike. I altered his face slightly to capture the image of First Mike in my head.

The fine hairs on the back of my neck began to rise. My fingertips tingled. The ring started to move, back and forth. I caught a whiff of an acrid, chemical smell. An unhealthy smell with the taint of something rotten underneath it.

He was coming.

The edges of my eyes began to water and my nose leaked and burned. I blinked for too long as the pendulum swung out, drawn as if magnetized, to the letter H. "Mike. Mike. Closer now." The odor intensified and my head swam a little, thoughts becoming unfocused. I think I shuddered, noticing the light growing dim, as if the bulb were dying.

The ring leapt over the pad. E. R. E.

The phantasmal fumes intoxicated me. I became detached from divining and yet scared that I might actually succeed. "Where are you?" I muttered under my breath and glanced around the room. Empty.

Then, my back grew so cold that I trembled. I turned around. When I saw him standing there, I almost fell off my makeshift seat. He looked the same as last time, with blood slowly dripping down his face. Only now, I swear I could hear its soft cascade onto the dusty floorboards.

"What happened to you?" My eyelids felt heavy.

He slowly reached up a hand and wiped at his nose, smearing his face and coloring the back of his hand red. He looked at it and his eyes went wide, in shock, and then he held it out for me to see. His lips parted but he remained silent.

Maybe this spirit couldn't speak. What were the rules?

But I knew one way, one very sure way, to find out what happened to him.

I stepped forward, lifting my hand. I hesitated a moment before letting my fingers touch the crimson streak he had made and I bit down hard on my lower lip. The pain anchored me, keeping me from being drowned by Mike's memories.

I'm in my room, reaching under my bed, and for the first time I notice my hands are smaller than they should be. I feel past old papers, clumps of dust, and a discarded sneaker to pull out a shoebox. I clutch it tight against myself. Even though I know what's inside, part of me is shocked, so much I almost draw back.

Then I'm down the stairs and out the door at a run. It's late afternoon and the sky is already growing dark. Cars are returning to the houses, their headlights winking as I run through the neighborhood.

I'm escaping the laughter of the jerks at school. Laughter at my worn clothes that aren't ever really clean. I'm trying not to think how Mother lets little Tracy run bawling around the house, her diaper filled with shit. I want to forget how Father works and works and barely spends time with me. What's inside my little box will let me do all that and makes me giddy with the promise of hours away from my life.

Blocks later, I take a worn path that goes past where they are building a strip mall. The last sight bothers me as I know it as a finished trio of stores, a greasy pizzeria, dry cleaner, and a convenience shop serving burnt coffee twenty-four hours a day, yet it is nothing more than a skeleton of concrete and steel girders.

I'm past it quickly though, and making my way through the woods. Even with night around the corner, I know my way to that fallen trunk covered in pale, sweating fungus. I cannot hear any sounds of civilization. All is deathly silent.

The earth smells freshly turned when I slide down to the trunk. The leaves feel cold beneath me. I sit down and lift up the lid of the box. Inside, there are no sneakers, but a stained paper bag, a sweat-

band, tubes of modeling glue, and a can of cooking spray. Mother never noticed it missing.

I've done this so many times before that it is almost a ritual. My fingers squeeze the end of one of the tubes, the clear glue coating the band. Even before I wrap it around my fist and lift it up to my face, the fumes burn my nose. I breathe deeply and when that first taste of light-headed wonder makes everything else forgotten, the side of my face gets sticky from brushing up against the band.

One of my hands starts twitching and I giggle at the spasms. My vision is wavering, and when I focus on my T-shirt, red dots appear on the cotton, like when you stare too long at the sun. More and more dots are appearing, bigger and bigger, until I lift the shaking hand and find my nose is running blood.

Trying to wipe my face with a sleeve unbalances me and I fall back, landing flat on my back. The ground is icy against my flushed cheek. I feel scared at how my heart seems to be stumbling inside my chest. All I taste is blood, the coppery tang choking my tongue.

Another giggle. I don't care that I can feel pain, along my arm until my entire left side throbs. My eyes are fluttering shut.

I found myself lying on the floor. The lower half of my face felt sticky and when I licked my lips I tasted blood. My nose still bled. When I rose up I felt disoriented and took deep breaths of the stale air of the shop, relishing the scent of dust and mothballs to that of modeling glue.

First Mike's spirit stared at me.

Poor First Mike. Dead in the woods from huffing. "In the woods," I croaked out loud without meaning to.

The ghost looked down at the Ouija pad. The makeshift pendulum slithered over to *YES*.

I remembered something Trace had once told me. Laying the dead to rest. Sometimes all it took was giving them a proper burial. "Do you want me to find you, Mike? Bring you home?" I talked to him like he was a child, keeping my tone gentle.

The pendant remained still but Mike's spirit slowly nodded. I pinched my eyes shut to clear my head. When I could stand without getting dizzy, I saw that he had vanished. I went to the shop's tiny bathroom. In the mirror, my reflection looked haunted: a face so pale as to be bone white, dark circles under my eyes, and drying blood under my nose and all along my chin. I washed off in the cold tap water, then took a rag and cleaned up where my blood had spattered the floor. When I was done, I felt an odd sense of satisfaction, even though my limbs dragged with exhaustion.

I knew what I had to do next. Tomorrow, I would find him.

Chapter 10

The next morning found me not at the shop but at the old hardware store across the street. I had never been inside the place before and asked the bespectacled man behind the counter where he kept the shovels. Would have been cool to buy an old-fashioned lantern like some Victorian grave robber, but I planned on digging up the body during the day.

The clerk didn't bother to look away from the tiny black-and-white television set. "Last aisle. Right side." His voice sounded ground down, probably from years of smoking.

Every wall, every shelf, was crowded with dusty merchandise in faded packaging. Axes, rakes, and shovels leaned against the wall. I picked a stout one with a wide scoop and thick wooden handle. It must have weighed twenty pounds. Leaning it against my shoulder, I walked back to the front. The man continued watching a football game while he made change.

Walking down the street with my new shovel left me with a sense of accomplishment. My plan seemed to be working. There had been no sign of Josh in the past two days. After the day's grim business was over, hopefully Trace would have forgiven me. First Mike would have been laid to rest.

I'd have to make sure that I cleaned it off and put it in my closet as a memento.

After all this business with ghosts was over, what then? I definitely wanted to be with Mike and see what happened there. But having a boyfriend meant I had to do something I had been dreading: come out to my aunt.

I refused to be like Liz, lying and hiding who I was. That way never ended well. I told myself Aunt Jan was cool; she really cared about me and would understand.

I would be all adult with her, sit her down and explain what had happened back home with my parents. Then I would promise to get my GED, offer to help out with some of the bills, prove to her I was responsible.

I played over the scene several times in my head by the time I reached Trace's house. Sometimes Aunt Jan was shocked at finding her nephew was gay, other times I envisioned her with this sly smile saying she knew all along. I imagined having Mike over for dinner so she could meet my boyfriend and she would take me aside and tell me how much she liked him.

Alongside Trace's car in the driveway was a black Corvette I didn't recognize. I rang the doorbell.

Trace gave me a slightly chilly greeting, obviously still upset at me, but her eyes widened a bit when she saw the shovel.

"Can me and my spade come in?"

She stepped to the side and I called out a greeting to Mike as I walked into the front hall. Would he remember me from last night? I could feel his presence in the house. Odd, how I never really noticed it before. Or maybe my newfound confidence in my abilities made me more aware.

"He's not here. Went to the mart." She folded her arms across her chest.

"Oh, I was saying hello to First Mike," I said. I noticed that she wore her "out-on-the-town" makeup rather than the usual "early weekend" face. I even caught the faint smell of perfume.

"Dare I ask why you are carrying a shovel? Smiling and carrying a shovel?"

Before I could answer, Taylor came out of the kitchen drinking from a coffee mug. He wore canvas pants with safety pins along the outer seams and a dark T-shirt with the caption *Honorary Fiend* in red lettering.

"Hey," he said and leaned against the far wall behind Trace.

I blinked and recovered from my surprise. I wanted her to come along with me to the woods, but Taylor's presence threw my expectations awry. "Uh, well, I was hoping you would come with me." I looked back and forth between them, deciding to be restrained rather than involve him with ghosts and all. "I have a little chore to do today."

"This doesn't lead to some midnight voodoo ritual, right?" Taylor said with a grin. "I promised my granmama no more of that shit. I've cut down to Santería."

I hoped he was joking. But then, Trace would like a boyfriend who practiced a little black magic.

"What's going on?" Trace asked warily and reached for the mug in Taylor's hands. He smiled as she took a sip.

I sighed. She seemed in no hurry to get rid of him. I regretted how quickly my earlier optimism turned to anxiety. She had left me with no choice but to out myself to him. "Last night I had a little séance."

Her dark eyes widened a bit. "Who with?"

"By myself. Well, with First Mike really."

She gave me a look, one I had never seen before. Her eyes narrowed slightly and one side of her mouth twisted down, showing teeth. I could not be sure what thoughts were behind it. "So tell me what happened."

"I saw him, Trace. I know what happened. His ghost showed me so much. I know how he died."

She opened her mouth to say something, then just as fast turned away a moment, hiding her face. I could hear the emotion in her voice when she finally spoke. "We're going for his body, aren't we?"

Taylor moved quicker than I did, placing his arm around her. For a moment, a flash of jealousy went through me. Shouldn't the best friend be the one who comforted her?

"It's the only way to let him rest. You're the one who told me that."

Trace hesitated a moment then muttered "Okay."

Taylor grabbed a leather jacket and offered to drive. His total acceptance without saying another word bothered me; I didn't know whether to be appreciative or irked. Even worse, my satisfaction at being able to release First Mike's spirit was rapidly diminishing. I had thought Trace would be happy at my plan but instead I seemed to have only made her more upset.

As we all headed out the door, I looked over my shoulder and called out, "Comin' along?" In the shadows of the kitchen, I thought I caught a glimpse of First Mike standing in the corner. I held out my hand to him but nothing moved. "Fine, I'll see you there."

We took Trace's car so I could sit in the backseat. With the heavy shovel lying across my knees, I kept leaning forward between them to offer directions based on the stolen recollections of First Mike's last afternoon.

"So, you can really talk to the dead?" Taylor asked me. Trace had started telling him about our ghost problem along the way.

"It's no super power." I pointed at the next turn.

"Most ghosts only want to be heard," Trace added. "After dying and being trapped in this world, it's like living a nightmare. They're so desperate to talk to someone they don't care whether the person—the medium— wants to listen."

"Still. That's pretty creepy," he said. I saw his eyes looking at me in the rearview mirror.

I shrugged. "Lucky me."

I yelled out to stop the car when the surrounding trees seemed familiar to my stolen memories. We got out and Taylor went to the trunk. He took out a rolled up plastic tarp and a flashlight. "Just in case we don't find him before dark."

The wind picked up as we started to trudge through the trees. The fallen leaves leapt and danced at our legs and more fell onto our heads. I led the way. I told myself that First Mike would want to be released. The notion sounded a bit hollow, though. Would I give up the presence of someone I deeply cared for, even if he was only a shadow of his former self, or be selfish and keep him around to comfort me?

I heard crunching footsteps quicken behind me and turned around. Taylor caught up to me.

"Hey, sorry if this freaks you out."

"Nah," he said. Then a moment later. "Well, a little."

"And this is the easy ghost." I chuckled bitterly.

"Listen, you guys should talk."

I looked at him, a bit confused.

"Trace and you. She's all upset. Over what happened the other day and now this has weirded her out a bit."

"She told you about me and Mike?"

"Not everything." He shrugged sheepishly. "But enough to guess."

I stayed quiet. I wasn't sure what to say to her or even how to bring up the topic.

"You know how lucky you are."

Again, I laughed. "The last thing I feel these days is lucky."

"Sure you are." He lifted a hand back toward Trace. "You're best friends

I'm just a boy she's liked for a few days. But you... you're the one she can talk to any time about anything. No secrets because they don't matter."

"But I did keep that from her."

He reached down and plucked a fallen twig from the ground. "You were afraid of hurting her. Happens. But don't let it break the friendship." He started peeling the bark from the stick, revealing pale wood. "I envy how close you both are. Me, well, because I like her, I worry I'll say or do the wrong thing."

His candor surprised me. My earlier jealousy turned to pure shame. "Thanks." If I wasn't so embarrassed I would have said more.

He smiled and threw the stick off to the side.

I turned back and waited for Trace to catch up to me. Wearing unpractical shoes, she was having a tough time walking through the woods. I offered her a hand, which she took without hesitation.

"I never meant to fall for your brother. Just... happened."

She stopped and caught her breath, pushing an errant lock of hair away from her face. "I know. Just seeing you both together was the last thing I expected. I never thought you'd be into him. I never thought he was gay."

I nodded. She left unsaid my past crush for Josh. While I still was a bit lost on how attraction works, I understood that love's something more than feelings happening overnight. Even with Mike, I was unsure if in the end we'd be together. Everything worthy in life, it seemed, was full of effort and doubt.

"Mike's sweet and likes quirky things. He's artistic. I never knew how much all that matters to me."

She blinked and I realized that her eyes were growing a bit teary. "You won't hurt him."

I was glad she stated rather than asked it. "Never." I hugged her tightly. "Not either Mike."

"We're doing the right thing?" Her face buried against my shoulder muffled her voice.

"This from the spook expert?" I had to laugh as I rubbed her back.

"It's different when it's happening to you. With someone close."

When had all the macabre things we used to love turned against us? I worried that we could never go back to that innocent pair reading obituaries to plan the afternoon.

"He wants to be found. I'm sure." I saw Taylor standing ahead of us, leaning against a tree. He seemed in no hurry. "By the way I like your boy."

She wiped her eyes and giggled a little. "Thanks. I'm glad you do."

We started walking together. I think more than memory led me; an almost tangible feeling guided me. When I saw the fallen tree, old and rotten, blocking a ditch, I knew we had arrived.

"This is it."

Taylor helped me climb down into the ditch. Moist clumps of dirt rained down from the twisted roots of the dead tree overhead. He handed me the shovel, then dropped down, landing on his feet, his back against the earthen wall. Trace stood above us.

I carefully scratched at the ground with the tip of the shovel blade. The soil resisted for an inch or so before turning easily to reveal the first hints of dirty bone: a hand, fingers loose and falling apart at the joints. I think we all held a breath. I dropped to my knees and used my hands to clear away the rest of the soil. I uncovered something hard, its sides corroded with rust. A can of cooking spray. But nothing more of First Mike. I dug deeper and found only grimy beetles.

"He has to be here."

Taylor slid down to the ditch and started turning over more dirt. "Here," he said and held up an old tube of modeling glue, squeezed empty and discarded.

Then Trace called out. It took us a moment to climb out. We found her a few yards away, kneeling over and gently brushing aside the fallen leaves.

"I thought I saw something like bone." She pried up from the ground a lower jaw. Several teeth were missing along the front, the sockets filled with dirt. The fillings on the back molars were still shiny. "Ugh."

"Think it was animals?" Taylor asked.

"Probably. Mike's been out here for more than a decade. They'll have to comb the woods all around here for ..."I looked over at Trace, who stared at the ground while hugging herself. "Sorry, hon."

"We better call the police and let them know we found a body," I said.

"We passed a gas station not too far back. They'll have a phone," Taylor said.

"Think I should stay here?" I looked up at Trace.

"No," she said a little hastily. "I mean, he's been here for years, he won't mind waiting a little longer."

I sighed with relief and rubbed my hands clean on my pants. I really hadn't wanted to stay around with the dead.

Chapter 11

That afternoon, I broke my promise never to step foot again in a graveyard. But I owed it not only to Trace and Second Mike but to their older brother to attend the funeral. Still, I tried to remain utterly silent. Even if I couldn't see any ghosts, some hidden spirit was within earshot.

The day was terribly windy and the first scarves of the season slapped people in the face. The clouds overhead had churned to an angry shade and there were umbrellas ready.

Mr. Vaughn had shaved but it only made his face look even more saggy. He bowed his head the entire time. Next to him, sitting in a wheelchair covered with a blanket, was a gaunt woman. I could see the resemblance to Trace and her brother even though their mother's skin was so taut over the skull and her eyes were deep within their sockets

Not many other people attended besides the small Vaughn family. A few kids from school. Maggie stood nearby, while Liz and Kim were off to the side. Every so often I would glance over and see Liz looking at Maggie rather than the casket; they had broken up a few days ago and I'm sure the wounds for both were raw.

Trace looked as if carved from ivory. Every so often she would lean to the left, tilting against Taylor who had not adopted anything more austere for the event than a black leather jacket over his normal punk clothes. When they took their place in front, Taylor had his arm lightly draped over her shoulder, but by the time the minister started reading it had sunk lower, pulling Trace close.

I stood next to Mike along the right side of his mother. His new suit looked sharp; I had to admit there was something to be said for modern clothes.

I never noticed before the overall sense of sadness surrounding funerals, a layer that hung over everyone, like a lead-lined overcoat. What little was said in low voices of those around me never reached my ears but was snatched away by the wind. The enforced quiet, both my own and that of the others, was disturbing in itself, but far worse were the screams that started when the casket lowered into the hard ground.

She startled us all. Her screams began low, guttural, almost drawn-out groans. Then the pitch rose, still sounding like a tortured single note. Wailing. You see the word, know what it means, but until you hear the sound of actual wailing, you cannot know that it's as much a cry from the heart as from the lungs.

Mrs. Vaughn tumbled out of her wheelchair, dragging her blankets along on the ground behind her as she scrambled toward the edge of the grave. She never stopped that horrible sound, even when the other mourners—her husband, Taylor, some graying cousin or uncle—rushed her. One of her thin-fingered hands, the nails bitten down to the quick, managed to reach the edge, scraping in the dirt. Then she was pulled back and her screams turned into barked words. Among them I recognized "No!" and "Mike!"

The attention turned to Mrs. Vaughn. Except Mike, who stepped closer to the grave and watched, silent, as they laid the brother he never knew in the ground. I ignored the brouhaha to stay with Mike. I noticed he was crying quietly. Not a sob or a shake or whimper. His tears rolled down his face and were wiped away by the never-ceasing wind. I caught one with a fingertip before it evaporated and he turned and I came so damn close to leaning down and kissing him then. Up to then I always thought it might be wonderful to hook up with a boy in a graveyard, a secret sin of sorts, but when the moment came, all I could do was think of the sadness of his as well as those around us. And so all I did was nudge his head with my own.

Rapping woke me. I looked up from the pillow. Someone was at the window. I rubbed the sleep from my face and pushed myself up. I saw a small pale face looking in and my chest grew tight as I held my breath. First Mike? Had we screwed up and now he was loose and angry like Josh? Then the face spoke my name and I recognized Second Mike's voice. I left the bed and undid the lock, lifting up the pane. Cool air rushed in.

"Mike, what are you doing?" I mumbled still half asleep.

He started to pull himself up and over the windowsill. I took hold of him underneath the shoulders and helped.

He had changed clothes and wore a clean white T-shirt and sweats. He looked freshly scrubbed, his hair still damp and a shade darker than its normal brown. Wearing dyed boxers, I shivered at the chilly breeze slipping through the open window, and the sudden, nervous thrill of being so exposed to him.

"I needed to see you."

"Okay." I walked back to the bed and sat by the pillows, bringing my legs underneath me.

Mike came over and sat down next to me. He kept his gaze down toward the floorboards. "Do you like me?"

I smiled at the innocent question. "Very much." As proof, I brushed my hand through his hair.

He sighed and leaned back a little so it was easier to reach him. "Good," he whispered.

"What's wrong, Mike?"

He turned his head and flashed me a smile. "I like it when you call me that. Just Mike." His eyes roamed over me, my face, and my bare chest. Then, blushing suddenly, he looked away.

"So?" I let my hand drift down to his neck. I wanted him to tell me why he had stolen away to visit me in the middle of the night.

"Trace told me about the ghost. The *other* ghost." His emphasis made it clear who he referred to. Josh.

I sighed. I couldn't really blame her. Mike deserved to know some of what had been happening to me of late. Only, now I felt bad that I hadn't been the one to tell him. Was I guilty of lying by omission?

But it had been almost a week since Josh had last come over. I was sure he was gone, probably returned back to 47.

"Yeah, he wasn't a good thing. I'm sorry I ever ran across him."

He turned around to face me and moved a few inches closer. We just stared at each other for several moments without saying a word. He looked small and nervous and I wanted nothing more than to hug him tightly against me.

He bit his lower lip. "Do you think that way about me?"

"No." I cupped his chin with my hand. "No regrets with you."

"I remember the first time I saw you. The night Trace first brought you home. Both of you were in the backyard and I watched from my bedroom window. I saw the little orange glow from your cigarettes dancing around. Then heard your voice as you started renaming the stars." He leaned in close to me and I slid my arms around him.

"That was so cool. Not the names, some were kinda weird. But the fact you told her everything about your new constellations. Just like someone from ancient times, you had your myths and stories." He looked up at me, his eyes sleepy. "After that, I always thought about you."

"And then you kissed me." I smiled.

Mike nodded. "I thought I'd die. Or maybe you'd spit or something 'cause I did it wrong. I never kissed anyone before that."

"It was the kiss I'll never forget." I leaned down and kissed him again, marveling at how his lips parted and little puffs of breath seeped from his mouth into mine.

"Feeling better?" I asked.

He blinked and buried himself back into my arms. "Yeah. Can I sleep here with you tonight?"

I almost growled out a "Yes" and pounced on him but the gentle way he had asked the question made me stop. Letting my hormones take over might not be the smartest thing to do. Maybe savoring Mike slowly, in slow doses, was the right choice, especially considering what had happened with my sudden sex with Josh. "Of course. Though I may want to have another kiss." And I did.

Mike murmured a lot in his sleep. Getting used to the soft sounds took a while and so I found myself constantly waking, looking over at him lying beside me, then drifting off. As I dozed fitfully, I never noticed the temperature. The room began to cool until the only source of warmth was the boy next to me. I pulled at the covers and heard Mike moan. A new sound, one odd enough to startle me fully awake.

What little light came through the window caught the wisps of my breath visible in the air. I turned my head and saw

Josh standing by the side over where Mike lay. As if carved from ice, he stared down without a hint of expression.

Before I could even react, Josh thrust his arm deep into Mike's chest until his hand had sunk to the wrist. Mike groaned a weak, pathetic sound. He twisted his limbs, freeing himself of the sheets but not Josh's touch. I could not help but notice the bulge in Mike's sweats and remembered how charged Josh's touch could be.

I sat up. Josh raised his eyes to me. They still shone blue but were empty, like those of a corpse. I shuddered, but not from the cold. Though his face remained vacant, his anger was tangible. I heard his voice though he did not open his mouth. "You want him rather than me. You're just like Roddy."

"Get away from him." Without even thinking, I grabbed at the arm just inches above Mike's chest. My hand didn't pass through Josh, there was no sudden rush of memories. Instead, my fingers found the solid softness of the well-worn letter jacket.

Josh grinned at me. Those perfect teeth flashed like a hungry predator's.

"This isn't about him. You want me."

Josh narrowed those dead eyes. "No." He hissed the word. "You should be wanting me."

"Josh." Parting my lips to lure him into a kiss, I leaned over Mike. Josh moved forward to meet my mouth with his own. Then I hit him.

I'd never thrown a punch in my life. I weigh a little over a hundred pounds soaking wet. But the need to get him off Mike, the fear that he was killing him, made me strike out. More fear than force was behind the blow when it connected with his jaw. When my hand sunk inside his head and the memories began, I had a moment to wonder—had I caught him off guard or had desperation given me strength?

Down in the rec room the Everly Brothers are singing off a 45.

Bye bye love, bye bye sweet caress,
hello emptiness
I feel like I could di-ie

*A couple of girls and guys dance in the center of the basement.
Arlene has already attached herself to another member of the team,
sharing her Coke with him. I look around and find Roddy standing
in the corner. Colin's next to him, leaning down so that he can hear
whatever Roddy's whispering to him. Roddy's soft lips practically
brush Colin's ear in a lover's kiss. My blood burns.*

*It takes seconds for me to cross the room. I've never crossed a
football field any faster. I don't wait for either to say a word to me.
No more lies, from them or from me.*

*I lift both hands and push Colin hard against the wall, feeling
satisfied when I hear the thump of his back against the wood paneling.
His glasses hang askew on his face.*

Roddy grabs my arm. "Are you nuts?"

*I look into his face like I've done so many times for almost a
year. I've memorized his features, from the tiny scar on his chin from
where a dog nipped him as a toddler to the exact shade of brown in
his eyes. But right now I see something new. Anger. I don't know
how to react to that.*

*"Why are you with this guy?" I shrug off Roddy. He is only a
wide receiver and not a good one at that.*

*"Not here, Josh." He speaks in a low voice and motions with his
head at the rest of the party.*

*I glance around. The music plays on but the room has grown still.
Everyone is staring at us. I've grown up used to being watched. Out
on the field, everyone follows my every move. All the girls, and some of
the guys, they watch me and want me. But here, I can feel something
different from their eyes. When did they start accusing me?*

*I fight the fear, turning it back into rage. My fist easily connects
with Colin's soft stomach, one quick blow that gives me the satisfaction of hearing air expelled from his lungs and leaves him hunched*

over for a second before falling to his knees. I want him to get back up again so I can throw another punch.

"You should be with me!" I scream at Roddy. He has to learn that he's meant to be with only me, his teammate all through high school, not some bookworm.

The other guys standing around us grab and pull me back. Seeing Roddy bend down to help Colin stand up, only makes it worse. A sneer crosses my face, seeing how the guy's eyes look ready to cry. "He's not a man."

"And you're acting like one?" Roddy adjusts the glasses on Colin's face.

"But I love you."

He looks visibly struck by the words. "Josh, no."

"Don't say that. You love me, not him." The arms that hold me drop away. "We should be together. I hate seeing you with him."

Roddy's face falls. Colin still has one arm around him and glares at me.

Someone close by giggles. I look around. The stares are a thousand times worse than before. One or two have their mouths open in shock. Arlene chews her gum and giggles again.

"Fuck you, Arlene." I snap at her.

"I doubt it, Wyle. Now we know why you never have."

Everyone starts laughing. At me. They've never done that before. I push them aside and run out of there. Out of the house and into the cool night air which feels good against my flushed face.

On the street I pass by Roddy's '51 Moonlight cream-colored Chevy. We had sex in the backseat of that car once. Right near some railroad tracks. I remember when the train hurled past the car and it shook and it had been the most amazing lay of my life. The next day, passing each other in the hall at school, I called out to him, "Choo, choo." He blushed and turned away. I loved that I could make him fall apart like that.

I kick in the car's right headlight and start running down the block. I don't stop until I leave the neighborhood behind and find myself walking on Rt. 47.

I keep my head down, my hands in the pockets of my letter sweater and try not to think what had just happened. By tomorrow, the whole town will know I am a faggot.

An engine's purr comes from behind me. I turn around and see a single, glowing white light quickly approaching. Roddy's car.

Josh vanished, leaving me to collapse on top of Mike. His body felt too cold beneath me. Worried that I was too late, I rubbed his skin, his limbs, moving myself over him to share my warmth. I wrapped the cover around us both and buried my face in the crook of his neck. I listened for a heartbeat, the sound of him breathing. Both were so faint, as if only echoes of life.

I tried to wake him, first by talking softly in his ear, then by lightly pinching his cheeks. He blinked sleepily. "Weird dream," he muttered and fell back asleep.

I went to the hall closet and brought back every spare blanket I could find, just like Trace had done for me. I woke him again and sat him up in bed next to me, covering us both. As he became warmer, he murmured happily and lay against me, wrapping his arms around my neck. I rubbed his back, feeling relieved he seemed okay—now that I had found someone as sweet and amazing as him, I was scared of him being taken away. I was even a bit mad, I admit, that Mike remained clueless how close to dying he had come.

I turned that anger to Josh. But it could not compare with the memory I had taken from him of the party. Josh's resentment and jealousy at Colin made my insides hurt. The shame of being outed could drive a guy to do the worst things. Had Josh's own boyfriend killed him?

Chapter 12

For the first time ever, I woke because a warm boy slid up against me, laying his face in the crook of my neck. Mike's soft breath teased my skin, and I purred and pulled myself closer to him. My hand, guided by hormonal instinct, knew to slip under his cotton T-shirt and rub his smooth back. Mike pushed himself against me then.

"Morning," he murmured in my ear.

I didn't answer. The last thing I wanted was for it to be morning and for me to have to get out of bed. Mornings are evil.

My hand left his back and slid to his ass, squeezing it once. Damn, I loved his sounds. So gentle. I had the urge to press further, slip my hand around the front and see what touching another boy there felt like. But then the house creaked and rudely reminded me of what had happened last night. That memory doused my desire and chased away sleep. I decided to keep the attack from Mike; I didn't want to upset him if at

165

all possible. What I needed to do was to talk to Trace and figure out how to end Josh's haunting. For good.

"You should leave before we get caught." I gave him a quick kiss. He moved in for another and another. I slid a hand to the back of his head, letting my fingers brush through his short hair a while as he nibbled on my lower lip.

"Yeah, we should." His murmurs tickled my ear and made me want him more. Damn. I could not stop myself from licking his chin, moving down to kiss his neck. He moaned softly, spurring me further. My hands found their way to his back and ass, rubbing in slow, tight circles.

He slowly ground his body against mine. His breath came in ragged pants.

I slid my fingers under the elastic waistband. The skin I found was soft like silk. Not really sure what to do, I just let my fingertips lightly tickle their way up and down between his small, rounded cheeks.

He groaned my name.

"Yes?" I asked softly.

"We should… we should…" His eyes were closed and he licked his lips, then he shook his head slightly. A few drops of sweat fell from his forehead onto my chest.

I suddenly felt conscious of how far we were moving. Again came concern of rushing Mike into something so seriously physical, not when I was just discovering how much he mattered to me. I quickly slid my hand out from his sweats. I wondered why wasn't I born with that tiny devil on my shoulder that cartoon characters possessed.

He looked up at me with one open and amazingly jade-green eye. "Thanks," he mumbled and just relaxed on top of me. Our breathing began to calm down and fall in sync.

"Let me see if the coast is clear." Wearing jeans and a shirt I found on the floor, I slowly crept down the hall. Was my aunt still home? I hoped she'd maybe left for the casinos or something.

No such luck. I heard sounds from the kitchen. Even worse than her being there was her home making breakfast. I had to get Mike out fast.

I found him already dressed and smoothing the folded covers. I stood in the doorway, blinking at the sight. He had made my bed. He had made my bed! I think that was the first time that had ever been done—I mean, no matter where I lived, the bed simply stayed perpetually slept in. Why bother to make it all neat when later on you would be spending hours tossing in it anyway? But the boy had actually given it definition, sharp corners, the pillow a space of its own. He looked up at me and smiled sheepishly.

"Uhhh…" I didn't know whether to thank him.

He walked into my arms. This new feeling, of embracing a boy when I wanted, was addicting. I wondered when we would be together next. But then I remembered Josh's attack last night. The ghost had to be dealt with before I put Mike in jeopardy again.

I took him by the hand and led him out of the bedroom. Just a few yards to the front door, the tricky part being the gauntlet past the kitchen. If we made a dash, maybe my aunt wouldn't see us.

But I forgot one important thing: my luck or lack of any. Just as we were passing the kitchen, the phone rang. I swore silently. My aunt reached for the telephone hanging on the kitchen wall, and saw us there in the hallway. She stopped. Then she recovered from her surprise with a slight smile. She wore an apron covered in what looked like flour. "Morning, mind answering that? I don't want the pancakes to burn."

Pancakes?! Mike smiled and whispered the word like it was almost holy. He went straight for the kitchen table. I groaned, leaning back against the wall, until the phone rang again. I reached to answer it.

My luck turned infinitely worse after I picked up the receiver. "Hello?"

No one spoke and in a moment I would have hung the phone up when her voice broke the silence. "What the hell are you doing there?"

Just hearing my mother curled my insides and splashed them with burned acid. I slammed the handset back onto the receiver, where it slipped free and dropped to the linoleum with a crash to spin around at my feet.

I knew my aunt and Mike had to be staring at me. My boy sat at the table with a knife and fork in hand, ready for breakfast. Aunt Jan stood at the stove, a spatula ready in hand.

Trying to hide my sudden fear and anger, I looked down at the floor.

My aunt walked over and picked up the phone, glancing at it casually before putting it back on the wall. "What's wrong? You're shaking."

I didn't answer her. The ringing began again. Only this time, the sound became an obnoxious alarm because I knew who was on the other end.

Without taking her eyes off me, she reached up and grabbed the phone. I closed my eyes and heard her say "Hello."

Aunt Jan's eyes widened. After a few moments she said, "So nice of you to call, Sarah. And yes, of course he's still here." Then she listened a while, her face wincing, undoubtedly from my mother screaming at her. "I hardly think of it as harboring a criminal."

She held the phone away from her ear and mouthed to me, "sit down," pointing next to Mike at the table. I did as I was told. I could hear the wasp-angry buzz of my mother's voice from across the room.

"Sarah, listen can I call you back… the pancakes… well, I don't want to serve the boys burnt pancakes." Aunt Jan winked at us. "Yes, I said boys. What's so wrong about… listen, I cannot talk to you like… no, let me say I won't talk with you yelling. I'll call later." She hung up the phone coolly and went straight to the stove.

I sat there with my head in my hands. This was all wrong. I had wanted to come out to Aunt Jan my way. Now not only had my mother cruelly outed me, but I had been caught with Mike. My aunt would never trust me again.

"They're a little brown, I'm afraid." Aunt Jan put a plateful of pancakes in front of Mike. "Do you want any?"

I shook my head no. "Did she call me sick?" That had been her favorite word for me in the last days at home.

My aunt put the pan into the sink and began to untie her apron. "Do you want any jam with those? There's syrup on the table."

"She thinks I'm this perverted thing, right?" I watched as Mike reached over my arm to grab the bottle of syrup. He didn't seem surprised that it was artificial strawberry-flavored gunk rather than Vermont maple.

She sighed. "Your mother has... issues. Always has. I don't know why she's mad at you."

"Mad? She's not mad. Mad is when you send your kid to his room without dessert, not when you tell him you want him out of your house!" I slammed my hand down on the table.

Mike looked at me with anxious eyes as he stuffed the first forkful into his mouth. A bit of the neon red syrup stained his mouth and trailed down his chin. The sight, so reminiscent of his brother's ghost, left me uneasy. "She really did that?" he said around chewing.

"Both of them did. They hate me, are disgusted at me because—"

The phone rang again. I never realized how irritating that sound was. No one moved to pick it up.

"Relax," my aunt started.

"They always ruin everything. I wanted to tell you before I had to run away. They would have tossed me out. I'm gay."

Mike dropped his fork. "Sorry," he whispered, blushing at the sudden attention the sound brought.

My aunt brushed her finger against the messy top of the squeeze bottle. She brought the finger to her mouth and grimaced at the taste. "Uhh, this is what, pure sugar?"

"Didn't you hear me?"

"I'm not old enough that I'm deaf." To Mike she spoke, "Excuse us." Then she looked at me and pointed out into the other room. We moved to the living room, while Mike went back to eating the stack.

"I heard you. What did you want, some wild response? For me to suddenly start screaming, to throw you out of my house?"

"No," I muttered. Ashamed for being so melodramatic, I couldn't look her in the eyes. I worried I had lost my place as her favorite kin.

"Confession time." She sighed and rubbed her forehead a moment. "A couple nights after you moved in, I called her. I know, you asked me not to, but when my nephew suddenly shows up on my doorstep and begs to stay with me, I worried what happened."

"You knew?" The knot that had formed deep in my stomach after hearing my mother's voice jerked a bit, but whether it started to loosen or merely pulled taut, I couldn't be sure.

From the kitchen Mike called out. I didn't know he could yell. "Ms. Kapel, would you have any milk?"

"In the fridge, just pour yourself a glass," she yelled back. "And he is?"

"Mike. Trace's brother."

Her eyes grew larger. "Am I wrong, or did he... sleep over?"

My head sank. Just when I thought I had a chance...

"Shit." She drew out the curse. "He's what fourteen? And you're only seventeen!"

"Mike's fifteen. And nothing happened."

She gave me a scathing, doubtful look.

"Honest." Again, a bit of exaggeration. I raised up both hands in defense. Adults love to suspect the worst.

"Does she even know?"

I could only shake my head.

She groaned. "Okay, well this has to bring a couple new rules."

I just nodded. Whatever she said, as long as I could stay.

"Number one, I'm not ready for any kid in my house to be fooling around. Relax, but think how awkward I'm feeling right now. So," she nodded toward the kitchen, "Mike can come over anytime but he ends the night at his house. Alone. Understood?"

Relief soothed my frayed nerves. I had worried she might say no boys at all or something. Instead, I felt treated like any other normal teen. How cool was my aunt! "Understood. No problem."

"Number two, no more secrets. You need to trust me and I need to be able to trust you, okay?"

I nodded. Still, I knew I would break this rule. I wasn't ready to come out to my aunt as a medium. For once, being gay seemed inconsequential compared to how complicated my life had become thanks to seeing ghosts. Plus, that would lead to talking about Josh, which would be trouble. For now, I had to lie to my aunt: what kid doesn't keep something secret from an adult?

"Let's finish eating and then we can take him to school." She rubbed her forehead a moment. "How come that doesn't sound right?" she asked with a nervous chuckle.

I hugged her. Tightly. "I love you," I said softly.

Aunt Jan squeezed me back. "Always remember, this is your home, too."

I had been waiting for that moment, for her to say those words, since I walked through the door. A ball of angst that had been inside of me for months broke apart, leaving me finally with one less worry. I finally felt at home.

I convinced my aunt to drop me off as well out front of the high school. Mike nudged me, his fingers lightly tickling my ribs before he ran off to get to class. I watched him open the glass doors of the front entrance. It had been months since I had stepped into a school. As I climbed the steps I remembered the teasing from other kids over how I dressed or looked or acted. I found myself hunching over slightly, as if to protect the vulnerable spots inside my chest.

The hallways were quiet and empty. My footfalls on the cheap floor tiles sounded loud. I had to find Trace but I had no idea of her class schedule. I passed a fire alarm and paused, tempted to pull it down and send everyone running. But didn't they coat the levers these days with some special dye that marked you as guilty?

I found the office. The woman behind the desk eyed me as if I could be dangerous. Powder caked her face and one badly penciled eyebrow arched higher than the other.

"I need to find a student. Tracy Vaughn. It's very important."

"Why aren't you in class?" She pursed her lips. Her face looked ready to spit out a particularly sour lemon rind.

"I don't go here." I waited for that to sink in. "Can you help me, please?"

"We don't give out *that* sort of information. Not with what's happening these days."

Okay, so, what? Any kid dressed in black is a terrorist? She's insane and thus worthless. I looked up at the clock. Every school in every town in the country must buy the same dull round white clocks from the same manufacturer. I had a couple of hours until lunchtime.

I went out to the parking lot and found Trace's car. Unlocked like I thought. I went inside and put the seat back.

I mulled over how to tell Trace about last night without freaking her out. Without boldly lying, which I refused to do, there was no way to avoid bringing up Mike sleeping over. I just hoped she would consider Josh the only threat to Mike. I hoped my boy wasn't in too much trouble for being late to class. I closed my eyes and envisioned him sitting down, listening so attentively. The thought made me smile and I could feel myself drift. After getting so little rest last night, I couldn't stop myself from falling asleep if I wanted.

A sharp rapping woke me. I nearly jumped. I realized where I was and looked through the glass to see a smiling Trace standing by the car. I rolled down the window.

"What's wrong? You're never out here."

I yawned. "What time is it?"

"Time for all good little boys and girls to go home from school."

"Aren't you a bad little girl?" I reached out to the textbook she carried. "Ugh, psychology. Good, maybe you'll have insight into my stalker."

"Josh? He's back?" she asked and tossed the book over my shoulder into the backseat.

"It's worse. Last night he went after Mike."

She scrunched her eyes. "Wait, that ghost was in my house? Is Mike okay?"

"No and yes." I slid over to the passenger seat. "You better get in."

Trace opened the driver's side door and sat down. "Tell me."

I brought my fingertips to my lips a moment and took a deep breath. Better to just say it, I told myself, and hope being blunt helps. "Mike came over after dark."

She stared at me but did not say a word.

"He wanted to talk," I continued, aware that, for once, I had no clue what she was thinking behind her dark eyes. That really bothered me. "It was late and we fell asleep together." I swallowed, my mouth dry from nerves. "We only slept."

"And what about Josh?"

The way she posed her question made it seem to me involving more than just last night. I thought she wanted to hear that I was over my infatuation with Josh and that any interest I had with her brother was something deeper. I hoped she would believe me that my feelings for Mike were vastly different than those I had with the ghost.

"I woke up in the middle of the night. Josh was there, by the bed. I think he's so jealous that he attacked Mike. I think he tried to kill him."

"So Mike's okay?"

I put a hand on her shoulder. "He's fine. I don't think he even knows what happened. I chased Josh off before..." I just couldn't say anything more.

"We have to put Josh down," she said. "Suppose next time you didn't wake in time?"

I nodded. "Yeah."

"I know only four ways to get rid of a ghost. Those that need a proper burial—"

"Like your brother."

"Exactly. But Josh took you to his grave so that's out."

I was happy to hear I would not have to be digging up more bodies.

"Some spirits need help performing an unfinished task." She glanced over her shoulder while backing out of the school lot.

"He never mentioned anything like that. All he wants is love."

"Or what he imagines love is."

"True." I wondered if Josh had ever understood that love was more than infatuation or wanting. Had he ever cared for Roddy? Or worried whether Roddy cared for him? "What's next?"

"Well, is there any object he's tied to? Something important to him that's a link to the material world?"

"Nothing I can think of."

She chewed her lower lip a moment. "That leaves exorcism."

"Oh, don't tell me I have to quote Latin prayers."

The edges of her mouth lifted in a near smile. "No. The book says that any medium can risk an exorcism—"

"Risk?" I didn't like the sound of that.

"Yeah. I don't remember everything but it involves entering the spirit's memories and convincing it to depart."

"I want to go back to that word 'risk.'"

She turned and looked at me. "There's the chance the medium could fail and experience the ghost's death."

"I'm guessing that's fatal or something."

She nodded solemnly.

I groaned. "Great." I looked out the window. The suburbs were filled with people that had no clue what went on around them. I was so envious of them. Envy's my game and I play it too well.

"Maybe there's another way."

My acute sense of gloom told me otherwise. "Maybe there's not. I'm not even totally sure what happened to Josh that night. All I got was a glimpse."

"We really need to find out more. Maybe one of the people from the party's still alive. We could go back to the library and get a list of his classmates—"

"Teammates. I think it was mostly the guys on the football team and some girls. And the boy Roddy brought." The more I thought about Colin the more familiar his face seemed.

"Think Roddy's still around?"

"I doubt it."

"What's wrong?"

"The last thing I gleaned from Josh was seeing Roddy's car approaching fast."

"You think his boyfriend ran him down?"

"Maybe." Did I really believe Roddy would do something so terrible? He had been outed by Josh, and back in the 1950s that had to be awful. "But still that's really fucked up."

We drove back to the library. Even though there was no sign of the ghostly librarian, I made sure to be absolutely quiet until we reached the second floor.

Trace slid the '57 yearbook over to me while she opened the following year. I paged through seeking Roddy and Colin. In the football team photo, a monochrome Roddy stood next to a smirking Josh. The tiny caption listed his full name. Rod Karden. As I thought, Colin wasn't on the team. He had lacked the build, being too thin.

I found him in the junior class photos. My jaw dropped, as I read his name. Fifty years had transformed Colin from a lanky kid with glasses and a bow tie into my distinguished boss. Malvern.

"Trace." I tapped the photo. "You'll never believe this."

She peered at the page. "Shit." Her eyes went wide. "No way."

"But Malvern's not gay! He's always chasing widows." Yet, even as I said that, I had to wonder. The man had never mentioned any wife. All his talk of womanizing could have been just a facade to conceal his real lifestyle. The fact that he had been a central figure in a huge drama that happened decades ago between two lovers left me unsure.

Trace shook her head. "I don't know what to think. Look," She slid over the '58 yearbook and showed me a memorial page to Josh. "Sort of touching when you think what a scandal his being gay must have been."

"Either they ignored it to appear decent or people really did care." I ripped out the page. "Could come in useful," I added, folding it up and slipping it into my jeans pocket.

We went through the rest of the '58 book but couldn't find a senior class picture of Roddy. He wasn't pictured or listed playing football, either.

"What do you think happened?" Trace asked. "Could he really have done it? Was he arrested?"

"You would think if that happened it would have been part of the local legend?"

"You're the one who thought Roddy was guilty. Maybe he just dropped out."

"So what, he ran to the border? This is Jersey, where would they go? Delaware?"

"Hold on." She left and in a few minutes returned with the local phone book. "What's his last name?"

"Karden."

She flipped through more of the book. "Okay, here's an R. Karden. 15 Earl Court."

"Sounds ritzy."

"It is. The neighborhood is old houses and money. Doesn't your boss live around there?" She ripped the page out. I winced at the sound, sure that the ghost librarian would come looking for vengeance.

"Okay, so now this is getting weird." When had a beautiful house in the suburbs become the reward for running over your boyfriend?

"We need to talk to one of them. Finding out what happened that night is important for the exorcism."

Earl Court had cobblestones rather than sidewalk and gigantic maple trees lining the street. Every three-storied house demanded our attention with eaves or gables or gingerbread trim.

Several cars were parked in the long driveway of number 15 and a few more were out front. Next to them, Trace's car looked more of an eyesore than usual, resembling a tumor on wheels.

"Looks like a shindig," I said.

"Want to bag it?"

"No, the more we delay the more things get risky. Besides, this may not even be him." Then I saw the antique red Thunderbird. "That car." I pointed it out to her. "That's Malvern's." I still found it hard to believe my boss was involved in all this.

We went up to the door. I was suddenly mindful of my shabby appearance. I ran a hand through my hair, hoping to comb out the snarls. I did not want to look like a scarecrow making a house call.

Trace rang the bell. Even the chime sounded expensive.

The thin man who opened the door had gray hair trimmed close to the scalp. He wore a powder-blue sweater and pale linen pants. He blinked at us through wire-rimmed glassed. "Can I help you?" We heard gentle laughter and light jazz tunes drifting out from behind him.

"A Roddy… Rod Karden wouldn't happen to live here?"

His eyes narrowed suspiciously. "Why do you ask?"

"It's extremely important we speak to him." Trace stepped forward almost into the house.

"I'm a friend of Malvern's," I quickly added from behind her.

"Of Colin's?"

"Yes, I work at his store."

He looked at us a moment—I wondered what we'd do if he shut the door in our faces—then said, "Come inside."

We stood in a foyer with a marble tile floor. To our left was a posh living room with a great deal of white furniture. On the right, partially opened sliding doors framed a dining room filled with seated people. We had interrupted a dinner party.

"One moment." He lifted up a finger. His dislike of the notion of leaving us alone in the house was obvious, and he looked back several times as he walked into the dining room. I lost sight of him after that.

"Look at that chandelier." Trace stared above us. "Is that handblown glass?"

The man returned with Malvern and Roddy, who I recognized from stolen memories despite his age. My boss looked ready to dash out the door. "Something wrong with the shop?" He grew panicked and almost spilled the drink he brought with him.

"No, no. Everything's fine. I just—I need to talk to the host."

"Do I know you?" Roddy asked. His features retained their handsome past, though the hair had thinned and the neck sagged.

"It's about Josh. Josh Wyle. You do remember him, don't you?"

Roddy paled and took a step back; the man who had opened the door reached out to steady him. The act carried an air of tenderness that left me sure they were lovers. Malvern lifted the glass he held and took a hefty swallow. Both their reactions made me all the more suspicious.

"I haven't heard that name in a long time," Roddy said.

"I know, I'm sorry, it's important."

He seemed to consider for a moment, then turned to Malvern. "Colin, would you mind telling everyone I'll be indisposed for a little while."

"Fair enough, Roddy." My boss held out his arm to Trace. "You wouldn't want an old man to go back into that rough crowd all by himself, now would you, m'dear?"

Trace looked at me with a nervous smile.

I wanted to tease her with comments of the wolf come calling at her door. "Have fun," I said. Honestly, the worst I expected was that they'd share a couple drinks. I wouldn't wager on who could hold their liquor better.

Malvern stroked his moustache with exaggerated bravado. "I promise to return her in good spirits."

I followed Roddy through the living room into a small study. Along one wall was a bookshelf of thick volumes. An old state flag, framed in a shadow box, hung on another. Roddy sat behind a desk and the other man moved to stand behind him protectively. Roddy gestured toward the other chair in the room.

"So what's this all about?"

I needed to be a bit sly. Roddy would never just out and out admit that he had run down Josh. "Have you heard the legend about the ghost that walks down Rt. 47?"

"Of course. Everyone in town has."

"So then you know that it is supposed to be your high school boyfriend Josh?"

Roddy tapped a fountain pen lightly against the desk top. "This is all old news. People have been claiming to see the ghost for decades."

"And you've never seen him?"

Roddy's brow creased. "Honestly? After we moved back to town—when was that, Tom?"

"Eighty-nine, I believe," answered the other man.

Roddy nodded absently. "Back then I went out there a few times. I never saw anything. It's just talk."

"Not true. I saw him." I leaned forward in the chair. "More than that. His ghost followed me home."

Tom's voice held a terseness to it. "I think we've heard enough of this. Whatever you're playing, it's in very poor taste."

"It's true."

"It's also not Halloween, young man," Roddy said, pointing at me with the pen.

I never expected them to believe me. Not without proof. I steepled my fingers in front of my mouth as I thought through all the memories eavesdropped from Josh.

"Do you still own that '51 Chevy? What was it? Moonlight Cream?"

Tom looked down at his partner. "Rod?"

"Shame about the headlight. Or was there more damage that night?" I added.

"Yes, that was my car." His eyes narrowed at me. "What did Colin tell you?"

"Nothing. I never knew you had a thing back then."

Both of them started laughing. "Me and Colin? Dating? That's absurd."

"But—"

"Let me tell you, Colin Malvern never met a skirt he didn't fancy."

Tom removed his eyeglasses to wipe at the corners of his eyes. "We never see him with the same woman."

While relieved that my boss, who I did care for, wasn't to blame for whatever happened between Josh and Roddy, I stumbled over what had happened." But Josh thought you were cheating on him with Malvern. The fight at the party…"

"Right. Josh Wyle was the most jealous guy on the planet. I remember he accused me of staring at the other boys in the locker-room showers. All Josh ever wanted to do was make out and talk about plays and bitch about the others." Roddy sighed. "He resented Colin and never understood that I needed a friend to talk to about everything else in life, what we'd do after we graduated. Josh could never look past high school. He was stuck in the moment."

"And still is," I said under my breath.

"Colin's mom owned the dress shop in town and was friends with the swishiest designers. Everyone at school thought he was gay. After that awful scene at the party, he was smart enough to sleep with the school tramp—"

"Arlene Pervis," I interrupted without even thinking.

He stopped to stare at me like I had stolen his memory instead of Josh's. "Yes. That's her. How did you know?"

"Cheerleaders are always memorable." I imagined a gangly, teenaged Malvern plying Arlene with *haute couture* from his mother's shop. Or maybe something that only looked expensive. My fondness for the man tripled.

"Tom." Roddy reached back to take hold of his partner's arm. "Would you go get me a glass of water?" The dismissal hung awkwardly in the air.

Tom covered Roddy's hand with his own. "Are you okay?"

I had trouble with the guilt over so visibly upsetting Roddy and had to warn myself not to like him just yet until I knew whether he was responsible for Josh's death.

"Yes, just a little thirsty."

Tom nodded. He glared at me long and hard before walking out of the room. I shrank in my chair a bit.

Roddy leaned forward. "Now, what is this really about?"

"I need to know what happened that night."

"Why?"

"I wasn't lying before. Josh's ghost is haunting me." I tried to sound sane and stay calm. "He's still consumed by jealousy. He tried to kill my boyfriend last night!"

"You expect me to believe that?"

How many more parlor tricks would I have to play?

"Maybe you should tell me what other television shows besides *Wagon Train* did you have *fun* watching with Josh?"

Roddy's mouth opened slightly and his complexion became white. "Th-that's—"

"I went to the library. I read the senior yearbook. You ran off. Why?" I couldn't bring myself to directly accuse him.

"Josh outed both of us in front of most of the football team and in-crowd. They looked at us like freaks. Think they'd have kept the secret?" He leaned back in the chair and rubbed his face as if wiping away the years. "My father would have beat me within an inch of my life. I had no choice but to run away to New York City. That's where you went when you were gay on the East Coast in the fifties. I found out weeks later that a drunk driver had struck and killed Josh."

"A drunk driver?"

The door to the study opened and Tom came back in with a glass of ice water.

"Didn't you read the newspaper files at the library?"

"No," I said, embarrassed at how shortsighted Trace and I had been. We had just assumed everything about that night and those involved. I felt awful for wrongfully accusing him.

"Thanks, love," Roddy said, taking the glass from Tom. He took a long sip.

"I'm sorry for bothering you. And for messing up your dinner party." I nearly toppled the chair standing up. Learning that Josh had been to blame and had been tragically unlucky on his way home, left me empty. How any of this would help me with the exorcism, I had no idea.

Roddy waved aside my apology. "All this talk about a ghost?"

I shook my head. "Don't worry about it." There seemed little reason to stay and cause more grief.

Tom opened the door and, together, they escorted me out of the study and into the dining room. Trace sat chatting with several seniors around the long elegant table. She sipped something bubbly from a flute glass. Malvern looked up and smiled.

"My boy, your princess here is simply delightful."

Trace thanked him with a kiss on the cheek which left the man blushing.

"I'll walk them out, Rod." Malvern said. He patted me on the shoulder fondly.

Once outside, my boss turned to me. "I don't know why you're both so interested in Josh Wyle. But let me tell you, he was a pompous ass that nearly ruined my friend's life."

Trace took out her car keys. "Malvern told me a little what happened that night."

He nodded. "Rod probably didn't tell you how devastated he was when he learned Josh died. It took him a while not to blame himself."

"How long has he been with Tom?" I asked.

Malvern rubbed his chin. "Nearly twenty-five years, I think. They met in New York while in line for a Broadway show."

"Aww," Trace cooed. She looked at me and rubbed my arm. "One day."

Malvern followed us to her car. "You know," he said to me, "if Roddy had a friend like her growing up, he would have an easier time coming to grips with being gay. You're lucky to have her." He winked before heading back to the house.

He knew! I didn't know whether to feel ecstatic over no longer having to hide my sexuality from him anymore or unnerved, wondering when he had learned the truth. Tonight? Weeks ago? Or had he always known?

"What a devil your boss is." Trace laughed.

"Yeah." I opened the car door. "So now let's go back to your place. I want to know everything about this exorcism. We're doing it tomorrow night." In some ways, my life was becoming less complicated. I just hoped I would live to enjoy the new-found openness.

Chapter 13

Trace hung up the phone. "Taylor will come tonight." She walked back into her bedroom, where I was reading the book on mediums. "I'm a little surprised you want him there."

"He didn't freak out when we went looking for First Mike's body," I answered, glancing up from the page. "Would be good to have someone level-headed around." I didn't have to say why there might be a panic. Both of us had read the book's warnings. Not every medium who tried an exorcism survived. The deaths were particularly nasty, mirroring the demise of the ghost; I'd be crushed, mangled, as if hit by that drunk driver too.

"So with Maggie along, that makes four. Four's lucky, like clover. Or four corners of the earth."

I put the book down and looked up at her. This was not going to be easy. "I'm considering a fifth."

"Not your aunt?"

I shook my head.

"Malvern?"

"No. Mike."

She sat down beside me. "Are you sure you want that? He's fifteen—"

"I should be the only one in danger."

"Even so, suppose things go wrong." She lightly struck my leg with her fist. "Do you want him to… to see that?"

"Hopefully nothing will go wrong."

She chewed a fingernail for a while. "When are you going to ask him?"

"As soon as he gets back from the flea market. I asked him to pick me up something from the oldies music stand there."

She got up from the bed and paced around a little while I went back to reading for the umpteenth time. "I feel like we should be doing something to prepare for tonight… I don't know… like, cutting our hands and becoming blood brothers."

"Blood sisters would be more apt," I countered.

"Stop being so blasé about it!"

"I'm not. I'm terrified, but it doesn't help to show it. There, now you know."

The guy behind the Formica counter at DeBevec's filled a mug with fresh coffee for me. I handed Mike a tall glass of mint-flavored cappuccino topped with whipped cream as he ordered. I hoped his lips would keep the smell of mint after he finished.

"This is a cool place," he said to me as I poured sugar and half-and-half into my coffee. He took a sip and a bit of the cream clung to the tip of his nose. With an embarrassed smile, he wiped it off.

"Yeah." I led him to the farthest table. I didn't want anyone to overhear us.

"So the guy at the music store at the mart told me that 'Bye Bye Love' was rejected thirty times before being made into an album. Then it became a number-one hit." Mike took another sip, this one more cautious. "He had this huge hearing aid in his right ear. Looked like something you'd see in a sci-fi movie.

"Is this our first date?" he asked without pause.

"Uh, sort of. Actually, no, I still owe you one." I warmed my hands against the sides of the mug. "Listen, Mike, something is going to happen tonight."

"With a ghost?"

"Yeah. That CD I asked you to get? It's for a special séance tonight." I felt so awkward and exposed telling him all this. I didn't want to upset him, but after seeing Trace's reaction, I doubted there was any way not to. "The ghost that's been haunting me has to be put down. I have to convince him and it's not going to be easy. I think it's actually dangerous."

"So what, you don't want me there?" His voice became all defensive. "'Cause I'm too young?"

"No. Nothing like that. And actually it would make me feel better if you did come along." I reached out across the table and took hold of his hand. I finally had my wish of bringing a boy I liked to the coffee shop, only now I didn't have the time to savor it. I sighed.

He squeezed my hand hard and stared at me a while before finally saying, "Count me in."

Well after dark, the five of us met outside of Malvern's. Maggie had picked me up in her Jeep. Taylor brought Trace and Mike. After I let us in, I made sure to lock the door to the shop behind me. I brought along a flashlight with fresh batteries. All of us carried props needed for the séance. Taylor whistled as I played the light over the shop.

"I'm surprised this place isn't haunted." He poked at a heavy overcoat.

Trace slapped his arm. "Don't joke." She had been on edge ever since this morning.

"Sorry."

We climbed the creaky steps to the attic.

"We need space in the middle of the floor. We'll sit around you, one at each cardinal point." Trace said.

"What will that do?" Mike asked.

Trace shrugged. "Can't hurt. The book says that the mediums don't exhaust themselves as much while contacting the dead if others lend their psychic energy."

"So we'll all have hangovers after this," Maggie muttered as she began shifting the larger cardboard boxes. "Ghosts or no ghosts, seems like the usual Saturday night for me."

Working together, we quickly cleared an area. Trace began setting up candles around the room, Taylor following her path with the flashlight's beam. For a moment I feared one would get knocked over and start a fire, but told myself I had other worries. Soon the attic was lit with a gentle light and smelled of vanilla.

"I brought the boom box," Maggie said and unzipped the gym bag she had brought with.

Mike handed her the CD. *Best of the Everly Brothers*. She looked it over and frowned. "Now *this* stuff is scary."

"It's mood music." I knew Josh would be on guard hearing the song, but also figured he would be drawn to it like a moth to a flame. No one ever resists what's bad for them.

Mike held out to me an old letter sweater similar to the one Josh wore. It still had the price tag. "Sorta musty for fifty dollars."

"It will do." I took off the jacket I wore and slipped the sweater over my head. Mike helped me roll up the sleeves.

"Just remember," Trace said. "He needs to know it's okay to pass on to the next plane."

"I'll convince him." I patted the page from the yearbook in my pocket. From what I read in the book, I should manifest within Josh's final memories with everything on me. Showing Josh the memorial would help persuade him that his actions on his last night alive had been forgiven.

Taylor patted me on the back. "Good luck."

Maggie gave me a thumbs up. "Kick his ass."

Mike hugged me tight. "Don't be scared," he whispered into my ear.

"I'll try," I said softly. "I promise to come back to you."

We played the music. They all sat around me, Trace to my north, Mike to my south, and Taylor and Maggie being east and west, respectively. I faced the wall and closed my eyes. It took a while to forget the danger and let my mind go blank. Even though I was calmer than before, my heart beat fast. I took several deep breaths, holding the air in as long as possible before easing it out.

"I'm going to bring him here," I told them. I waited a moment. "Josh." I pictured him in my head, walking toward me on that lonely road. Even after all that he had done, all that I knew about him, I still could not help but admire his beauty. "Josh."

The room soon grew cold. I was thankful for the sweater.

"Josh," I said again.

I heard a gasp. It might have been Maggie.

I opened my eyes and saw him standing at the edge of the room, staring at me.

"Shit." Taylor muttered.

I dared a glance at Mike who stared at Josh angrily. It made me smile. Jealous boyfriends.

"Josh." I stood up.

If he noticed the others, he gave no sign. He took a step toward me. "Why? Do you want me now?"

A pang of guilt stuck in my gut. I seemed to always be lying, and no matter that it was for the best, I felt bad over it. Still, I nodded to him and spread my arms wide, waiting for him to embrace me.

He hesitated. I thought he would refuse, angry over what had happened the other night. But then he walked forward. I wrapped my arms around him. I envisioned a door opening and walking inside the night Josh had never forgotten, nor escaped.

Vision was the first sense that returned to me. I was on a landing. I could see Josh sitting down on a carpeted floor of a staircase landing. Across from him, leaning against the wallpaper, Arlene Pervis twirled her red hair in her fingers and smiled at him. I think Trace once told me that when girls curl a lock of hair in their hands, they're thinking about sex. Seemed silly at the time, but the expression on Arlene's face could not be doubted.

I tried to touch something. The banister. But I had no hands. I wasn't flesh. All I possessed was sight.

She leaned forward and took the beer can from Josh's hand. It looked odd, so different from the aluminum cans I was used to. This looked like thick tin with a cone nozzle on the top. When she brought the beer to her garishly pink lips, she made the act of drinking almost obscene as much as sloppy. A slight trickle of amber liquid escaped her mouth. The giggle that followed as she wiped her mouth with the back of her hand sounded phony.

I could hear. Another sense. I reveled in its return, trying hard to listen.

Josh turned away and looked down the stairs. Music came from below. I only caught a hint but it sounded familiar.

"Josh," Arlene said and nudged his penny loafer with her foot. "I'm wearing the school colors."

Josh turned back to her. "No, you're not."

The yearbooks I had looked at had been bound in green and rust. Her fuzzy sweater was white with pale blue trim and the pencil-slim skirt just a shade darker. Her clothes captivated me; I was thrilled to be seeing them in such pristine shape. She probably bought a new outfit just to wear for the occasion, I thought.

Arlene giggled again. "Yes, I am," she said softly and began lifting up the edge of her skirt. Her painted eyelids lowered seductively. "Underneath."

Tramp, I thought. Or maybe Josh did. Did it matter? Josh rose up a bit unsteady. He must have had more than just a few sips of beer.

"Here, let me help you." She grabbed hold of his hand and pulled him toward her. He obviously didn't want to kiss her. Arlene's lips pressed against his. I caught myself staring, remembering the first time he had kissed me. Some part of Josh would always haunt me.

Josh pushed her off him and rushed toward the first door, slamming it shut behind him.

Though sure she could not see me, I still gave her a shrug. Then, by wanting it, moved myself through the bathroom door. It felt like I drifted more than walked.

"Josh, are you okay?" Arlene said and knocked a few times.

Josh was bent down over the toilet bowl throwing his guts up.

Another sense returned. The sense of smell, though this one I was not so keen on experiencing. Slowly I was aware of growing more distinct, more present. Focusing on myself, I could actually feel the floor beneath my feet, and yet I did not seem quite real. This was how ghosts experienced the world, a detached sense of self, always distant, being never truly in sync with their surroundings.

Josh flushed and went over to the sink, turned on the faucets, and splashed water on his face. When he looked up, he gave a shout. I saw only my own reflection in the mirror.

"Josh, you're scaring me," Arlene called out.

He turned around and seemed to finally notice me there. He stared at me. I offered a nervous smile.

"It's okay," he called out to Arlene finally. "I just need to be alone a moment."

"I'm here." I said it to myself as much as him. "I want to help you." My voice sounded like a whisper.

He shook his head at me, then went back to the sink and cupped a handful of water and rinsed out his mouth. He dried his face and hands on a towel.

All my rehearsals of what to say to him had fled my memory. I struggled to think of something on the spot. "Josh, none of this matters."

"I think that beer was skunked. Why my uncle drinks that Blackdram crap I don't know."

"This is going to be hard to accept. But… you're dead."

He narrowed his eyes at me. "Bombed more likely."

"No. I'm sorry, but it's true. Look, see." I reached for my pants but my fingers passed through my legs. Fuck! I tried again but I was as insubstantial to my own body as everything else.

He opened the medicine cabinet. Frustrated, I tried to shut it, but my hand passed right through.

What now? I had to convince him to move on but how? He'd never believe anything I would say. He was too stubborn.

He took out a bottle of Old Spice aftershave, one that had been on pharmacy shelves for decades. He uncapped it and took a deep sniff. His eyes closed and he got a dreamy expression on his face. But only for a second. Then his eyes opened and I could see how sad they were. He squeezed them shut again and gritted his jaw.

This was all happening so fast and right on cue. I stood in front of the door even though it would not matter. "You need to calm down, Josh. Hear me out." But even as I said that, I knew it was pointless. Josh was too worked up over Roddy and Colin. He smashed the bottle into the mirror which shattered loudly. Shards of glass fell into the sink.

Damn. If only he would stop being jealous, just for a moment. Then none of this would have to happen. He would never get into that fight, never run off, and never be hit out on 47. If only I could do the impossible and change the past….

The idea came to me in an instant. I didn't need to alter history, only how Josh believed it happened. A plan started to unfold in my mind. "You're overcome with jealousy. Calm down. Talk with him."

"Oh, I will."

He threw open the door and took the steps down two at a time. I followed, feeling more like I glided than ran after him. "He should be with me," I heard him growl.

Down in the basement I heard that song from the Everly Brothers playing.

Bye bye love, bye bye sweet caress,
hello emptiness
I feel like I could di-ie

I never truly listened to that refrain before. The image the words conjured chilled me. Couples danced in the center of the basement, the rec room. I wished I could have spent hours watching them unseen. The guys had their hair slicked back with Brylcreem. Some of the girls had pixie hair, cut short with pointed bangs, while others had styled hair long with ends curled forward. I wanted to peek under the girl's full skirts to see if they wore crinolines.

Arlene had attached herself to another member of the team, sharing her Coke with him. Josh saw Roddy standing in the corner. Malvern... Colin next to him, leaning down so that he could hear whatever Roddy whispered to him. I looked hard to my boss's younger self, trying to see his future old face in the smooth, thin features. With his thick tortoiseshell glasses and uptight button-down shirt, he seemed more likely to hang out in a library than a bar.

Josh's face, meanwhile, had grown ruddy with anger, he gritted his teeth. He moved his athletic build swiftly, it took only seconds for him to cross the room. He lifted both hands up and pushed Colin hard against the wall, grinning at the thump the boy made when he hit the wood paneling.

Roddy grabbed his arm. "Are you nuts?"

I came up behind Josh. "Stop this. He only cares about you."

But Josh ignored me. He stared into Roddy's face. "Why are you with this guy?" Josh shrugged off Roddy's grip.

"Not here, Josh," Roddy said in a low voice and motioned with his head at the rest of the party.

The music played on but the room grew still. Everyone had stopped and turned to stare at them. Even I could feel the many accusing eyes.

Josh's answer was a fist to Colin's stomach, one quick blow that left him hunched over and falling to his knees. "You should be with me," Josh yelled.

The other guys standing around grabbed Josh and pulled him back. Roddy bent down to help Colin stand up. The boy seemed ready to cry.

Josh sneered. "He's not a man."

"And you're acting like one?"

"But I love you."

Roddy looked visibly struck by the words. "Josh, no."

"Don't say that. You love me, not him." The arms that held Josh dropped away. "We should be together. I hate seeing you with him."

Roddy's face fell. Colin still had one arm around him and glared at Josh.

I wanted to avert my eyes, feeling so bad for not only Roddy but also poor Josh. I didn't think he had any idea what he was doing. His rashness, his shortsightedness, would not only end his own life, but, from what Malvern suggested, almost ruin Roddy's.

The faces of the teens around us were blank. The stares were a thousand times worse than before. One or two had their mouths open in shock. Arlene chewed her gum and giggled again.

"Fuck you, Arlene."

"I doubt it, Wyle. Now we know why you never have."

I winced. The others started laughing. Josh looked as if he had been the one punched in the gut. He pushed them aside and ran out. Out of the house and into the cool night air.

I drifted after him. On the street Josh passed Roddy's '51 cream-colored Chevy, a beautiful piece of machinery that I instantly wished I could take a ride in. That was a car any romantic would want to make out in.

Josh kicked in the right headlight. Bits of broken glass fell. Shards passed through my intangible legs onto the street.

He started running down the block. I called out to him, but he would not stop.

I knew where he was headed. I caught up to him on Rt. 47.

Josh kept his head down, hands in the pockets of his letter sweater. "By tomorrow, the whole town will know I'm a faggot."

"That's not the end of the world." I said without thinking. But it was for him; the irony wasn't lost on me. I had run away too. Now, though, I wondered, what would have happened had I stayed? I doubted the whole town would have cared that one kid was gay.

"Tell that to my parents, my friends. They're all gone."

An engine's purr came from behind us. Josh turned around. A single, glowing white light quickly approached. Roddy's car.

The car slowed down once its light caught Josh. It pulled up alongside. The passenger window slowly rolled down as Roddy coasted beside Josh. He leaned over, still gripping the wheel. "Josh, get in the car."

"Listen to him," I said.

"Leave me alone," Josh muttered.

"You don't really want that," I said. "Trust me."

"Please, Josh. I want to… I need to talk to you."

Again I moved in front of Josh. This time he seemed to take notice. "How do you ever expect him to listen to you if you won't even give him a chance to speak?"

Josh stopped, looked at me, and then at Roddy, who put the car in park and slid over to open the passenger-side door.

Yes, I thought. This should do it. Get them to talk, Josh had time to cool off, they were bound to patch things up enough for the night. All I need is for them to get back together for just one night.

"So where is he?"

I groaned. Not a good way to start, Josh.

"Not here, isn't that what matters? Let me take you home."

Josh didn't budge. I wanted to push him into the car but my touch would have been no more effective than the breeze.

"Josh, it's a long walk back," I told him. Longer than you'll ever realize, I added to myself. "Go with Roddy."

But Josh didn't budge. He stood there with his arms folded over his wide chest. "Promise me you won't see him again. I'll get in the car if you promise me that."

Both Roddy and I called out, "What?"

"If you love me you'd do that for me. If he doesn't matter to you."

"Colin's my friend." Roddy's face grew flushed. "That's all. I won't drop him—"

"Not even for your boyfriend?"

"Not even. And if you really loved me, you wouldn't ask."

"Fine then. Keep him. But you're losing me." Josh slammed the car door shut on Roddy's anguished face.

"Josh."

Josh started walking again. Roddy pulled the car around and headed back the way he came.

"No!" I called out. "No! You asshole, you don't even know what you just did!"

"Sure I do. I just broke up."

"Listen to me. Get off the road. Cut through the woods. Take a nap. Just get off the damn road!"

"What does it matter?"

"You're going to get killed!"

He shrugged.

"Please, Josh."

"What does it matter? No one cares if I die."

I wished I could show him the yearbook page. "Not true. I care." I heard another car approaching. Was it the one? "If you die, Josh, I die too. And everyone that cares about me will be hurt. All my friends, my aunt, yes, my boyfriend, too, are going to be crushed."

I saw headlights in the distance. "Like I'm about to be crushed. Like Roddy was when you died."

He looked over his shoulder at me. "I doubt that."

The headlights grew closer. They weaved a bit on the road. The guy's driving like he's drunk. It's the one.

"Listen to me for once. Roddy was all broken up inside. He lost his first love. You never forget that. Never. Just hearing your name brings back the memories. I know he never stopped loving you even though you turned your back on him."

He stopped and turned around to face me. I could see the sadness, lit by the oncoming car's lights. "He never stopped?"

The car came crashing toward us. I could see by its light my shadow on the pavement. I could feel its oncoming heat. I was solid! I was real!

Josh did not scream.

Something acrid made me blink. I found myself lying on the attic floor. Everyone huddled over me, with Trace holding a tissue that stank to my face.

"Ugh," I weakly waved her hand away from me. I felt like I had been hit by the car, aching all over. I stretched my limbs a bit. Nothing seemed to be broken, just aching.

"So?" asked Mike. I noticed he had dark circles under his eyes. I glanced around and they all looked as bad as I felt.

"I don't know," I answered. Maggie and Taylor helped me sit up. "What happened here?"

"The ghost floated around you." Taylor said.

"Yeah, we could see your mouth moving but no words came out. That was a while and we all just watched not sure what to do," Mike went on. "Then you screamed and the ghost disappeared. You fainted and so Trace got some cleaner and we used it like smelling salts."

I reached out to him, pulling his head forward. He seemed a little surprised but responded by holding the back of my head and kissing me back.

"Enough making out." Trace pulled us apart. "Did it work?" she asked.

I looked around. More than that, I felt around. The attic was empty. I gave her an exhausted grin. "What's the chances my luck has finally changed?"

Epilogue

Halloween Night

The werewolf howled, its jaws wet with slaver, its claws bloody except that the movie was black and white and the yak fur pasted onto the actor seemed pretty dry. Trace walked in front of the television set just as the creature was bounding off through the foggy moors. Her black feathered wings drooped slightly, probably from when Taylor had pressed her against the hall wall, making out.

"Want some popcorn? Extra salty." She held out a very full bowl.

I nodded.

My aunt's house was decorated for the holiday, with all the bulbs switched to orange lights, crêpe-paper bats hanging from the ceiling, and the jack o' lantern Mike had made me sitting prominently on the coffee table.

The doorbell rang. Maggie, dressed as a construction worker complete with greasepainted five o'clock shadow and monobrow, answered. From where I sat on the couch, I could hear young children call out "Trick or treat!"

Maggie handed out candy. Valomilks. She shut the door. "One cute little boy was dressed as Snoopy." She opened a pack of candy. I had lost count how many she had eaten. "He's gay."

I smiled instead of laughed. I hadn't uttered a word all day, not even a sound. They all knew why. I was scared that some spirit might hear me and come calling. Halloween was just too risky.

Since the séance, I hadn't seen even a glimpse of Josh. I guess at the end, he realized something about love. I hoped he was truly gone and had not returned to his eternal walking alone. I didn't plan on finding out the truth.

Since that night, I had yet to see another ghost. But I didn't think I was cured or anything. It was only a matter of time before I ran across another one. I tried not to dwell on that, but ever since, I found myself talking less and less as Halloween approached. With my aunt out on her first real date in ages, my friends had decided to come over and keep me company. I was glad to have them.

Mike came back from the kitchen with two mugs of hot chocolate spiked with peppermint schnapps. He handed me one and then with his free hand lifted up the papier-mâché mask he had spent days on: A red devil with brown leather handlebar mustache. He sat down next to me.

"I love your costume." He took a sip of his hot chocolate.

I looked down at myself. I wore my normal basic black. I gave him a quizzical look.

"Just you, silly."

I smiled and leaned in real close, so close that my lips brushed against his ear. "I love you back," I said softly. I hoped he was the only one who heard me.

One-fifth of the author's royalties will be donated to: the *Gay-Straight Alliance Network*, which is a youth-led organization that connects school-based Gay-Straight Alliances to one another and community resources; and, the *Trevor Project*, a nonprofit endeavor established to promote acceptance of gay and questioning teenagers, and to aid in suicide prevention in that group.

About The Author

Steve Berman has been writing stories both queer and strange for many years. He has had more than 80 stories and articles published and his work has appeared in the young adult fantasy anthologies *The Faery Reel* and *The Coyote Road*. Mr. Berman edited the anthologies *Charmed Lives, So Fey* and *Magic in the Mirrorstone*. He is an active member of Science Fiction & Fantasy Writers of America. He once worked as a professional bookbuyer to expand his personal library and he now lives in Southern New Jersey, surrounded by many old and odd books.

CPSIA information can be obtained at www.ICGtesting.com
Printed in the USA
LVOW12s1619100615

441946LV00006B/670/P